CLOUDY WITH A CHANCE OF COWBOY

SAINT CLOUD, TEXAS
BOOK ONE

OLIVIA SANDS

DO YOU LIKE SURPRISES?

If the answer is yes, then go to :

https://oliviasands.com/e/

to sign up for Olivia's newsletter and receive exclusive previews, special promo opportunities and be informed of new releases.

BLURB

Can an outsider find love and acceptance in a small town?

When video game designer Chris Davis moved to the small town of Saint Cloud, Texas, to set up his company's new headquarters, he didn't expect to meet the beautiful bed and breakfast owner Cassidy Norton.

But can a relationship blossom amidst the tensions between the locals and his team of quirky coders?

From moonlit horseback rides to hot-blooded brawls, this funny and romantic tale brings tech and tradition together in a battle for connection.

CHAPTER 1

*D*ays like today were not what Chris Davis was used to so early in the year. Back home, parts of the mountains would still be covered with snow. Warm days like this would have come along in June, maybe not even till the Fourth of July.

Shaking his head, he adjusted his hands on the steering wheel. "Grow up, you big baby," he chided himself as he turned off the dirt ranch road toward town. "Besides, it's not like you moved to New Mexico or something. Now *that* would have been hot. This is home now."

As he came over the long rolling hill, he had to admit his best friend and business partner's hometown was the perfect place to call home. From this spot in the road, he had a bird's-eye view of Saint Cloud, Texas. The small town stretched out in a shape that some people called a banana and others preferred to call a smile. Either way, their own bit of heaven. He had to agree.

Though, Chris thought of it more as a smirk. The west side of town curved upward, following the "line" of the lips created by the Rio Plata that bisected most of the town. He was coming in on the inner curve of the Northside, the neighborhood that traditionally housed those ranch hands who didn't live on the cattle ranches that had once been the biggest economic engine in town.

Turning left, he drove through the Northside toward downtown, thoroughly charmed by his surroundings. Rio Plata Drive was lined with cottage-like small single-family houses, sprinkled with splattering of bright-colored flowers, children's toys, and the requisite small-town front porch rocking chairs. He loved the lack of self-contained subdivisions he thought had made people more insular and isolated. Instead, the Northside homes meandered through the neighborhood with all the streets either leading to Rio Plata Drive or to Schneider Boulevard. Unlike big cities, there were no convenience stores or fast food joints to interrupt the decorative line of homes.

Reaching the historical downtown, Chris parked by Saint Cloud Fire Station. Firefighters were in front washing two of the bright red trucks. Chris fought hard to resist the temptation to check out the fire engines. As a kid, he'd fantasized about being a firefighter, riding in to put out the rising flames and save the day for a family who could have lost their home. Life had led him on a different path.

Today, he had things to take care of. Reaching into the back seat of his pickup truck, he pulled out the leather briefcase that, in his mind, looked so out of place.

Dressed in jeans and a button-down short-sleeved shirt, he had to ask himself, what was he doing carrying a thousand-dollar briefcase? But for now, it was all he had.

Chris, his brothers, and, of course, Simon, his best friend and partner, the reason they were all here, were eager to start their new lives. After filing the quit-claim deed, he moved on to the next thing on their to-do list, delivering the septic system inspection report confirming the property was not a health and safety hazard to inhabit.

"Now, just a reminder," the clerk smiled at him, "out that far, there's no city water. Most folks like you are on a well."

He nodded.

"And there's no trash collection."

"And what exactly do we do with the trash?"

"Well, when you have enough, you take it to the dump. Keep in mind folks are more eco-friendly here. You'll want to learn about composting. If you need some help, you can ask The Happy W or the Bar-X. Two of our biggest ranches; they'll have plenty of information for you." Looking left then right, she leaned forward and lowered her voice. "You want to make Justin Logan mad? Mix some plastic into his composting pile."

"Got it." Though Chris had no idea what to do with the insight.

The woman sat upright again. "Very well then. Welcome to St. Cloud."

His tasks for the city completed, Chris headed upstairs for the other reason he'd come into town—to "press the flesh," as his brother Andrew liked to say. Honestly, Chris wished that Andrew had been the one to take care of this, but Chris had the time while his brothers handled other matters.

On the second floor, he found what he was looking for: a door with a brass plaque. Engraved on the plaque, new enough that the edges of the engraving were still machine-shop sharp, was *Kimberly Johnson, District 1.*

Chris pushed the door open, surprised to find that there wasn't an outer office, just … an office. "Hello, Miss Johnson?"

The blonde woman stood up. She was the first person Chris had seen who was wearing a suit. A red jacket and pencil skirt highlighted her trim figure. Her hair hung to just below her shoulders, reminding him of a polished television newscaster. Chris was sure the professional look came off well with her constituents and in public appearances. "How can I help you?"

"Hi, I'm Chris Davis." He took a step forward. "We just bought the Cloud 9 ranch, and I figured I should stop in and make my introductions."

"Well, now," Kimberly said in a drawl that Chris was still adjusting to, "that's very nice of you, Mr. Davis."

"Chris, please. My brother Andrew is the eldest, so he gets to be Mr. Davis." He shook her extended hand. "He's tied up with other matters today."

"The Cloud 9, huh?" Kimberly held up a finger. "I don't want to be rude, but you mind if we go down the hall? I think Mayor Jones would love to say hello himself."

Knowing the amount of money that the newly formed Cloud 9 Games company had already dropped in town, he wasn't surprised by her request. He followed Kimberly down the hall, this time to an office that actually had a secretary.

"Marcy," Kimberly said as they came in, "is Tom around? This is Chris Davis, one of the folks who bought the Cloud 9."

"Oh, he's around." Marcy waved a hand at the door. "Go on in."

Tom Jones? Chris had to bite back a chuckle. Tom Jones was one of his grandmother's favorite singers. A little surprised at the casualness of the way city government ran on the second floor of the Saint Cloud City Hall, he appreciated the access it seemed to give him.

Behind the desk, a man in his mid-fifties with a slightly balding head and enough fat on his neck to be considered plump if not quite double-chinned, spoke on the phone. "Now Jaime, I get what you're saying—but that campaign song's been working for going on twenty years now. I don't see any reason to get rid of it. Besides, like you, I'm not looking to go to Austin. Surely the lieutenant governor can put up with one remix song when he swings by for a rally, see what I mean?" The mayor nodded at the phone and smiled. "Sure, sure. I'm not lookin' to be the main event. I'm just sayin' it'd go a long way toward my feelings if it could be played before I made my introductory remarks... Right, right ... Hey, I got some business to take care of. We can jaw this over later. Right. *Adios, amigo.*"

The mayor hung up, and Kimberly spoke. "Tom, I'd like to introduce you to Chris Davis. He's one of the new owners of the Cloud 9 ranch."

"Well, now, I've heard somethin' about that!" The mayor stood and offered a hand. "Tom Jones, mayor of Saint Cloud. How're you doin'?"

"It's a pleasure, and I have to say, you've got the most efficient city hall system I've ever seen." Chris shook hands with the mayor. It was a politician's handshake, and Chris noticed that the mayor's smile didn't quite reach his eyes. "Seriously, where'd you get that system?"

"Oh, my son did a tour in the Air Force, was stationed over in Japan." Mayor Jones sat back down. "Married a local girl, and when he came back from his deployment, seemed all he could talk about was how good their city offices were. Used a bunch of words that I don't remember, but anyway, seemed like a good idea. Folks like it well enough."

"Considering you keep getting re-elected, I'd say so," Kimberly quipped. Based off of just a few seconds, Chris could catch the vibe. Kimberly Johnson wasn't content to be just the city council member from District 1 forever. But apparently Tom Jones was an institution unto himself in Saint Cloud, and she wasn't going to rock the boat with the mayor unless she had to. "Anyway, Chris stopped in my office, and I thought you'd like to say hello."

"Well, sure, I've got time for that." The mayor's eyes tightened slightly. "Especially when I hear that not only are you buying the largest ranch in the Big Land, but you're bringing with you … a video game company?"

Chris nodded, knowing that the subject would have to come up eventually. "That's right. I'm a partner in Cloud 9 games, which is a brand-new venture, but also a partner in Big Sky Games. We're the publishers of *Sky Adventures.*"

The name made an impact, and Chris knew why. The game had started off as a project between Chris and his best friend Simon Smith, a class project for a freshman-year computer science class. But what started off as a five-minute demo had grown larger and larger, to the point now that *Sky Adventures* was talked about in the same breath as games like *Final*

Fantasy, Assassin's Creed, and even *Fortnite*. It had made Simon, Chris, and his brothers legitimate billionaires.

"I've got a nephew who plays *Sky Adventures*," Kimberly smiled. "Listening to him go on and on about it, I'm still not quite sure what type of game it is."

"The easiest way to describe it would be a role-playing adventure game," Chris smiled with pride. "But we've really expanded on the idea to be much more."

"That's all good, and I'll say I'm glad someone bought the Cloud 9 ranch," the mayor, who obviously wasn't a video game guy, nodded. "That's a darn good property that's been sitting empty for too long. But y'all aren't from around Saint Cloud —what brought you here?"

"Actually, we do have a connection," Chris chuckled. "One of my partners, and best friend, Simon Smith, grew up here in town."

"Simon Smith … say, isn't he Pattie Smith's boy?" Tom asked.

Chris nodded.

"Shame what happened to her, the way the cancer got to her so quick."

"I agree, but Simon felt like it was a blessing that at least it was fast, and she didn't suffer for long."

"True. So Simon convinced you and your brothers to come to Saint Cloud?"

"He did, but it's not just my family moving here. Simon and the rest of the company will be relocating."

A satisfied smile spread across the mayor's face. "Good. Good. How many people do you expect this little project to bring?"

Chris almost choked on the mayor's understated estimate. Obviously, the man thought a game studio operated with two or three guys pounding out a game on their computers in someone's garage in a few months. "Well, a multiplayer online game like Sky Adventures requires a good-sized team. Right now we've got two hundred people working on just the follow-up to *Sky*."

"Two … hundred?" The mayor showed more surprise than Chris was sure he intended. "Mr. Davis, that's a lot of new folks in town."

"They won't be all moving here at once." His words didn't seem to do much to ease the concern on the mayor's face. Chris wished once again that Andrew was here instead of him. But Andrew was dealing with the business operations and getting contracts signed. This conversation was on Chris, and he knew he'd have to lean on his own strengths to assuage the mayor's certain fears. "I assure you that we discussed the implications thoroughly before choosing St. Cloud."

"Two hundred," the man mumbled.

"As I said, this will not happen all at once. Simon made it clear that this is the sort of town that … well, you're a slice of Americana here. The sort of place where you can get to know your neighbors and get along with them pretty well, too."

"Most of the time," Kimberly bit back a chuckle. "Wait until you see how things get when the high school football teams play each other."

"I'm actually looking forward to it." He'd heard about Texas and their football, Friday Night Lights and such. "But my point is, while we would like to at least establish an office here in Saint Cloud, maybe even make Saint Cloud the headquarters for our company, we're not looking at shaking things up. We want to work with City Hall any way we can."

The mayor nodded, his face relaxing a little bit. "And by that ... you boys looking for any handouts, tax breaks, stuff like that?"

"No sir," Chris shook his head. "Although a few introductions would be nice. We plan to start operations at the Cloud 9 ranch, keep things self-contained. We were hoping you might be able to introduce us to the right contractors and local companies who can get the work we need done."

"Is that so?" The mayor slowly bobbed his head.

Chris didn't want to promise too much. "We want the Cloud 9 to not only be a working ranch, but a great place for business and, some day, a place to raise families."

"You're married?"

"No, none of us are," Chris admitted with a chuckle, "although we're not confirmed bachelors in any way. Although my brother Brian is a bit of a ... ladies' man."

"So you're looking at starting with the ranch." The mayor leaned back, looking more relaxed. "And then?"

"Well, that's where I know Andrew would need to work with you." Chris cleared his throat. "I'll be honest, Mayor, I'm the design and story guy of the business. So I can't make a ton of promises about company details; that's Andrew's field. But what I can promise you is that we want to keep Saint Cloud a great place to live and that Andrew will definitely make sure any and all projects are by the book. Permits as required, full approval of city engineers, and if necessary, town council too. In the meantime, you or any city official is more than welcome to come out to the Cloud 9, get a look at what we've gotten done so far."

The mayor seemed reassured and nodded. "I think I just might. I haven't been out there in … Well, Kimberly here might remember them, but she'd have been little. Long ago, when the Cloud 9 was the biggest ranch on the Big Land, it used to host community events. They were famous for their barn dances."

"I remember those; I'm not that young, Tom." Kimberly offered the man a respectful smile. "I caught one or two at the big barn when I was in school."

"The big barn. A real barn ?"

They both nodded.

He was pretty sure he knew which building they meant. He and Simon had discussed turning it into either another "house" for them to share or to turn it into a family recreation area, with space for a gym, a "man cave" for his brother Dylan, and more. But plans could change. "I didn't know that, but I think, with a little help, we could get those going again. No offense; I've never done a Texas-style dance before."

"Well, they're not that different from …?" Kimberly let the question hang.

"Colorado," Chris answered.

"City or country?"

"Country-ish." Chris grinned. "Grew up driving four-wheelers and have ridden horses enough to not make a fool of myself, but big town enough that I count my movie theaters in the multiple screen cineplexes. So while I've never really square danced, I've pulled off a line dance or two. If that counts."

The mayor laughed. "Well, with your clean-cut good looks, I'm sure there's a few young ladies around town who'll be willing to teach you." The mayor pushed to his feet and extended his hand. "Thank you for coming by, Chris. I'm sure we'll be seeing each other soon."

Sensing his dismissal, Chris stood up and shook hands with the mayor before following Kimberly out the door.

"The mayor's a good guy to be friends with," she said quietly as they headed for the stairs, "and I hope y'all can work together well. Saint Cloud could use a big business hub, and while video games may not be cattle ranching, good business is good business. You mind if I swing by myself?"

"Just wear jeans; the big house is in rough shape still."

Kimberly nodded. "Will do."

"See you around, Miss Johnson." Chris headed downstairs but stopped at the bottom when he heard his name called. Looking over his shoulder, a young woman, also about his age, descended the stairs in a pair of fresh blue jeans, a white blouse, and, for some reason, strangely by what he'd seen in town, black Air Jordans.

"Chris Davis, right?"

"Yes?"

The woman offered her hand. "Hi, I'm Amelia Hernandez, the city council member for District 3 … Do you have a minute?"

Chris checked his watch and, thinking about the rest of his goals for the day, nodded. "I'm clear at the moment, Miss Hernandez. What's up?"

Amelia looked around and shook her head. "This will take a little more time than just a chat on the steps. Would you be willing to have coffee? I'd like to talk with you about what you might be able to bring to Saint Cloud *beyond* barn dances."

"You've got good ears."

"No, what I've got is the office next to the mayor's and a shared air conditioning vent," Amelia chuckled. "What do you say?"

Chris thought for only a second and nodded. If anything, having another potential ally on the city council would be something Andrew would appreciate. "Sure. When?"

"I have an important meeting in thirty minutes. How about noon?"

Chris nodded.

"Great. There's a little B&B just about a half mile away at the corner of Rio Plata and Tower Street. Big blue house with a sign out front called the Cloud B&B."

"I'm sure I can find it." Chris pulled his phone out and held it up. "Self-proclaimed video game nerd. I'm also a whiz at GPS."

Amelia laughed. "You strike me as more than a video game nerd. See you at noon."

"Noon." He dipped his chin. "Thanks, Ms. Hernandez."

Amelia shook his hand again, and Chris turned to leave. Outside, he looked around. He still had two hours to kill and didn't feel like going back to the ranch. It was time to explore his new hometown.

CHAPTER 2

The alarm clock jolted Cassidy Norton rudely out of her sleep, an occurrence that had become far too common over the past few months. She could remember a time not that long ago when she was able to wake up before her alarm, refreshed and energetic—if not always eager—to take on the challenges of the day.

It might have only been months ago by the calendar … but to her spirit, it felt like an eternity. She knew she wasn't getting enough sleep, that her body and her mind needed refreshing.

But what also needed refreshing were the sheets in three of the rooms. Running a ten-room bed and breakfast wasn't a job that waited around, and there were other things to prepare.

Cassidy quickly washed her face, putting on some lotion before pulling her long, black hair into a ponytail. She knew she really should go down the street to Becky's Salon; her ends were looking split and harsh. But the ponytail hid most of the flaws, and if it got too bad, she could use some of the conditioner she kept in the rooms to give herself an ad-hoc deep treatment. Maybe she'd throw in some of the olive oil that she had in the kitchen. It'd be appropriate, considering that Great-Gramma Norton was Greek.

But the blue-gray eyes that stared back at her as she touched up her lip gloss were a gift from her mother. The steely gaze of a Scandinavian sky. She reminded herself that it was another sign of the strength in her heritage and that she could deal with whatever came her way.

Cassidy headed downstairs to the kitchen, where she was glad to see that both of her brothers were already up. The Norton twins, as they'd been known since starting kindergarten at Dusty Bend Elementary, were three years younger than her. She knew without them she'd have never been able to keep the bed and breakfast running.

"Morning," Tim, who was technically the younger by seven minutes, greeted her. Six feet tall and with the same black hair and blue-gray eyes as his sister, he was still the same lean two hundred and twelve pounds he'd been when he was a terror of an outside linebacker for the Schneider High Red Devils. "How'd you sleep?"

"Not enough to turn down that coffee I smell you boys got brewing," Cassidy said with a little chuckle. "Which one of y'all do I thank for it?"

"Me today," her other brother, Carl, said. Identical to Tim, he was about fifteen pounds leaner, the result of his football career being cut short. It was one of the two easy ways people could tell the Norton twins apart now, the other being the line of a scar on Carl's jaw. The result of a bar fight that had been Carl's rock bottom.

Cassidy was still helping him up from there, and while most people didn't give him enough credit for it, he'd come a good way since then. "Thanks, Carl." She glanced at the "silver bullet" coffeemaker and dispenser. "Think you can get a bullet going for the breakfast?"

It wasn't really a question. Cassidy was the boss, plain and simple. Tim might also have finished college, but Cassidy was the big sister. That counted for a lot in a town like Saint Cloud. Still, Cassidy had never been the type of big sister to boss her brothers around unless she had to. And Carl was better handled using a gentler touch anyway.

"Yeah, no problem. How much you want? Half bullet?" Carl asked.

She considered the contraption for a moment before shaking her head. "Just a third, there's only three rooms today, and I don't want to drink until I'm sloshing."

"Don't have time for that." Tim was right. All three of them were putting more sweat equity into the B&B than they'd like at the moment and had been ever since taking over the place. But that was what was required, and around Saint Cloud, people didn't complain about sweating. "So what do you need done today?"

"After breakfast, I want Carl to strip the checking out rooms, get them turned over. We don't have reservations for them, but I want them ready."

Carl nodded, accepting his work without complaint. Most of the time he was like that, which she appreciated. "Tim, I need you to take the truck over to Costco, pick up the weekly shopping. I'll get you a list after breakfast, and after that, the trim on the east side of the building needs looked at."

She knew what she was doing, giving Tim the "tougher" jobs while Carl got to stay inside, under closer supervision. But while Carl had picked himself up from rock bottom, he still had a ways to go before she entrusted the family credit card to him. And getting up on a ladder was sometimes painful for him.

Nobody complained, though; that wasn't her family's way. Instead, after finishing their first cups of coffee, they got to work. Breakfast was a two-person operation, Carl and Cassidy cooking up a basic but filling breakfast of eggs, toast, and sausage for their guests. Cassidy herself only indulged in an egg and a slice of toast, the cash register in her head totaling up the dollars and cents for each bite, even as her brothers ate with the hearty appetites that she knew they earned with their hard work.

After prep was done, she went out to the front desk, double-checking the computer while writing up Tim's shopping list. Every week it seemed to be a new challenge, how to shave a few more cents from every purchase. Gone already was the high-quality organic coffee that her parents used when they ran the B&B, replaced with bulk store brand coffee that came in giant tin cans and cost a third of the amount per cup. Gone was milk, replaced with non-dairy creamer, and gone were the pancakes. Not because pancakes were difficult or expensive, but syrup definitely was more expensive than toast and margarine.

Unless things turned around, she'd have to swap out the nice double-ply toilet paper for single-ply institutional rolls. As she was finishing that up, the first of the checkouts came in to settle the bill. "How was everything?"

"Great," the customer, a man from Oklahoma, said. "Every time work sends me through this part of Texas, I'll stay here when I can. Y'all are great."

"Thank you kindly," Cassidy tapped away at the computer. "You want to leave that on the card you reserved with or change payment methods?"

"Nah, card's fine." The customer adjusted the baseball hat he'd just put on. He touched the brim in a sort of salute, picked up his bag, and left. Cassidy took a moment to silently cheer on the charge without acknowledging the other side of the ledger and went back to work.

After getting the other two rooms checked out and sending Tim off with the truck, she got to work on her own task for the day: the rocking chairs. The Cloud B&B was in one of Saint Cloud's oldest buildings outside downtown, a rambling hundred-year-old clapboard building that had served first as a saloon—with rumors of the other activities that young, single cowboys indulged in happening upstairs—then a boarding house before becoming a hotel. Her family had owned the building since the sixties, fighting off the encroachment of chain motels and even folks jumping in on the AirBnB craze.

They'd done their best to keep certain expected country traditions. Like the rocking chairs. Handmade, they'd sat on the wide porch that ran the length of the east side of the building for as many years as she could remember. A pleasant spot to have an afternoon chat with a neighbor or just get out of the direct sun. Still, the morning sun was brutal on the old wood, and Cassidy knew they needed to be refinished. Which was her job.

Taking a plastic drop cloth down to the far end of the porch, the corner that was nearest to the back parking area, she spread it out before wiping her forehead. It was a good, clear day, not quite the sort of blazing hot that it would become in a couple of months. Still, she knew that by the time she went in for lunch and to check on Carl, she'd have sweat through her blouse and be ready to change into something cooler for the afternoon.

Carl would have happily done the job, and Cassidy trusted him to do it. But every late spring, one member of the family would be responsible for sanding and refinishing the rocking chairs. Her father had done it. Her mother had done it. And when they were old enough, Cassidy and her brothers had done the same thing. The year before had been Carl's turn. Next year was Tim's turn. This year was hers.

Using the deceptive strength that came with a lifetime of work, she carried the first two rockers down to the drop cloth and got to work with the scraper, taking off any chunks of last year's finish that had cracked and bubbled. Regardless of what kind of sealant the family used, it almost always happened. Next was the sanding. The year before, Carl had been able to do all six chairs in two days by using the old belt sander that had been in the basement. But the belt sander had given up the ghost over the winter when they'd had to redo the dining room table, and the budget didn't call for power tools.

After using the scraper, Cassidy took out the first sheet of sixty-grit sandpaper, quartering it to a good hand-sized chunk before running it back and forth over the roughened wood, paying careful attention to the armrests and seat. She honestly didn't care if there were a few rough spots on the legs, as long as the wood was sealed properly. It was slow, shoulder-aching work, and soon Cassidy could feel sweat trickling down her neck to soak into the collar of her blouse. "Don't whine, girl," she told herself as she switched hands to let her left shoulder take over for a bit, "this is cheaper than that gym over on Schneider Avenue that gets all the winery folks."

She was talking to herself, and she knew it. But she'd always been that sort of person, chatting herself up whenever she needed a bit of encouragement. She'd done it her entire life, even in school, where she'd often gotten shushed for talking her way through tests. About three-quarters of the way through the first rocker, the cell phone that served as the B&B's business line, as well as her personal line, buzzed. Cassidy reached for the phone, hoping it was a notification from the online booking sites, or maybe someone texting the B&B directly looking for a reservation.

No dice. Instead, it was Amelia Hernandez. Cassidy liked her. They didn't always see eye to eye on politics, but Cassidy had still voted for her when she'd been up for re-election because Amelia cared about the people in her district. She'd gone to every house, every business, to talk to people. More importantly, Amelia *listened*. So even when she and Amelia disagreed, they disagreed respectfully. A welcome change from the reality show craziness that was wider politics she'd see on TV.

Cassidy opened Amelia's message, smiling a little. *Think I can use the dining room at noon for a work coffee?*

That was another reason Cassidy liked Amelia. She was sharp, and she knew that the Norton B&B wasn't doing well financially. So if she was asking to do a work coffee at the B&B, she had an idea in mind. What it was, that was up to Amelia to reveal in her own time. She was a master poker player, but Cassidy knew that Amelia's intentions were good.

Sure, she sent back. *You want lunch too?*

Nah. Don't go out of your way, although if the coffee's fresh I'd appreciate it.

Appreciate it. Cassidy was a smart enough woman to read between the lines. Pull out a few extra stops, and it could lead to some business for the B&B. Cassidy was curious as to what that business could mean, but she'd find out soon enough.

In the meantime, she still had an hour and a half before she'd have to put the coffeemaker on. That was time she could get the first rocker's sanding done and maybe get the second one scraped down too. Work didn't stop for coffee.

CHAPTER 3

*C*hris pulled into the parking lot of the small strip mall across the street from the B&B, putting his truck into park. The strip mall was your typical sort of place, with a Korean grocery market, a bodybuilder supplement store, a barber shop, and a dry cleaner.

None of those interested Chris, although his brother Dylan did like Korean food. Chris figured he'd eventually get to know the neighborhood. He checked his watch and saw he still had about twenty minutes to spare. Walking along the sidewalk in front of the shops, he didn't see anything special that caught his attention, so after reaching the dry cleaners, he turned to look at the bed and breakfast across the street.

It was a large, older building in a sort of style that told Chris a lot about its age. At least a hundred or more years old, the two-story building had a wraparound porch that stretched from front to back. He could imagine the building being an Old West hotel or maybe a saloon. If a person took the time, an old building like this probably had volumes of history, and Chris didn't doubt that the owners could share a few stories to entertain guests. Still, at the same time he could see the building could use some TLC. The wooden sign out front looked a bit dingy, dusty at the creases in the carving and looking like it could use, at a minimum, a power washing if not a full repainting.

The lawn was in the same condition; good enough but just slightly worn, with a few dandelions and other weeds peeking up, including through one of the cracked flagstones that led from the sidewalk up to the front door. The stairs squeaked slightly as he climbed to the porch, even though he could see all of the nails were pounded down. He suspected the board was warped. A few screws might help, but a new board was probably better. At the top he opened the screen door and stepped into the reception area, his body immediately thankful for the air conditioning that cooled the sweat on his forehead.

The same as the outside, the room came with a ton of character and strong, solid bones. But at the same time, he could see where careful maintenance and care could no longer mask certain things, like the worn track on the carpet runners over the hardwood floors. Runners that had seen possibly decades' worth of shoes, boots, and luggage. Then, there was the way certain updates had been done, like how the Internet cables weren't run behind the walls or in discreet-looking channels but just held to the wall with industrial staples. Not ugly per se, but a setup that could look better with a bit of investment.

Chris walked up to the desk and looked around. Not noticing anyone, he dropped his hand on the old-fashioned bell. The clear tone rang out in the almost silent room. "Hello?"

"Just a sec!" a woman called from another room.

A second later Chris felt like he'd been socked in the gut.

Hurrying through the doorway, dressed in clean, simple jeans and a green blouse, with long black hair that hung behind her in a simple but elegant wave, she was absolutely beautiful.

The woman approached, going behind the desk. "Sorry about that."

Blue-gray eyes shone under naturally long, thick lashes, and he couldn't find his voice. All he could do was nod.

"I was just wiping down the dining room." She gave him a smile that dazzled, even if it didn't reach all the way to her eyes. Eyes that looked tired, and ... was that worried? A look that made Chris want to reach out, to sit this woman down, and talk with her until he could make all her worries disappear. Not a good idea.

Clearing his throat, he forced his mouth to move. "Chris Davis."

"Cassidy Norton." The woman seemed confused.

Chris realized he'd just announced himself but still hadn't explained why he was there.

"Do you need a room? All our rooms come with memory-foam mattress toppers. You'll sleep like a baby, and tomorrow morning we've got a complimentary breakfast from seven o'clock to nine."

"Ah, no ... sorry." And to his surprise, he meant it. Obviously, they needed the business. "I'm here to have coffee with Amelia Hernandez ... strictly business."

He wasn't quite sure why he'd said that last bit, but at the same time he was. He didn't want her to think he was interested in the council member, even if Amelia was pretty. But

25

compared to Cassidy? Nope. In his mind there was no comparison at all.

Cassidy's smile brightened a little, even if he'd just turned down her sales pitch, and she pointed in the direction of where she'd come from. "You're a bit early, Mr. Davis. Luckily, like I said, the dining room's nice and clean. How about you come on in; I'll get some fresh coffee on while you're waiting."

"No offense, Ms. Norton, but coffee in this heat isn't quite my thing." He smiled to soften his words. "Do you have some ice water or tea?"

"Got plenty of both, but I know Amelia—that woman runs on pure caffeine, and if I don't fill her tank up she's going to just collapse like an unplugged robot," Cassidy chuckled. "But you're right, it is a bit warm, so she'll like some iced coffee. How's that sound?"

"Don't go to any extra trouble, please."

Cassidy waved it off, and he noticed she wasn't wearing any rings. Maybe it was for work, but he hoped not. "No trouble at all. I've got some in the kitchen. I'll be back with a glass in just a minute. Go ahead and take a seat in the dining room."

Much like the rest of the house, this room was sparkling clean but had, no doubt, seen better days.

"Here you go." Cassidy came back carrying a small tray with a tall glass of iced coffee and a spoon. "Hope you like your coffee sugared?"

"When it's cold, for sure." He stirred the tall glass for a moment, gathering his thoughts. "Is this your establishment, Ms. Norton?"

"More or less." Cassidy shrugged. "It's a family thing, but my name's on the paperwork. What about you, Mr. Davis? What brings you to our little town? Wine?"

"No, although I heard that there's some fine wineries in the area." As he set the spoon aside, his manners suddenly kicked in. "Won't you have a seat?"

Cassidy thought for a moment, nodded to herself, and pulled out a chair across from him. "There. Now your neck won't get a crick."

He laughed softly. Beautiful, helpful, and a sense of humor. "Thanks. Now, as for your question, my company is moving to town. We just bought the Cloud 9 ranch."

"The Cloud 9, huh?"

He nodded.

"You talked with Justin Logan or Amanda Munoz yet? They're your neighbors and own the biggest working ranches in the county."

"Not yet. We've been busy settling in. Anything I should know? They get along, or did I just drop in between the Hatfields and the McCoys?"

Cassidy laughed, shaking her head. "They get along well enough, mainly because they respect each other's different businesses. Justin's ranch, the Bar-X, is a real working ranch, raising beef. Amanda's ranch, the Happy W, is more of a dude ranch. They'll sell cattle from time to time, but they're more about … well, tourists."

"I see," Chris smiled. "I'll make sure to say hello then."

"You into cattle, Mr. Davis?"

"No, and please call me Chris."

"Chris," she repeated quietly.

For just a second, his mind went blank at the sound of his name on her lips before he remembered what they were talking about. "Actually, I'm in business with a friend and my brothers. We do video games and intend to make Saint Cloud the headquarters of our new company."

"Ah … and that's why Amelia wants to meet with you here? She doesn't want to talk business with you where you live, in Kim Johnson's district. So video games, huh? And Saint Cloud?"

"My partner, Simon Smith, is from here. He really pitched the town. Made it sound ideal for our plans. So far I think he's right. Hopefully when my brothers get here next week they'll see it the same way."

Cassidy nodded and took a sip of her own glass of iced coffee. "Me too. So what do you do for the company?"

"I'm the story guy, the creative one. My friend Simon is the genius who makes my ideas happen. My oldest brother Andrew's the nuts and bolts operations guy, my brother Brian's Mr. Charisma, which in our business means he handles the PR because he could sell ice in Antarctica, and then there's Dylan, who's trying to figure out where he fits in the business."

"How did all those brothers let an outsider in?"

"Outsider? Oh, you mean Simon." For a moment the question had thrown him. Ever since they'd met in college, Simon had been such a big part of his family that Chris often forgot he wasn't legally part of his family. "Simon might not be a brother by blood, but he's a brother nonetheless."

"That's nice." Her smile brightened and this time reached her eyes. "What kind of games do you design, anyway? Shooters? Fighters?"

"Nah, our current one is a role-playing adventure game," Chris said. "Don't get me wrong, there's plenty of fighting and shooting you can do, but there's a bit more reason to it than just folks taking potshots at each other."

"I like that idea," Cassidy said, and Chris swore he could see her check him out. He knew he wasn't an unattractive man; back when he'd been an undergrad, he'd had no shortage of female company even if he was majoring in computer science.

But in his mind, he'd never seen interest from a woman as stunning as Cassidy Norton. He opened his mouth to ask her about herself, but before he could, the door to the B&B clapped open. "Cassidy? You here?"

"In here, Amelia!" Cassidy said, shaking her head as if waking up from a bit of a dream herself. "I was just entertaining your guest!"

Amelia came in, and again Chris compared the two. Now, Amelia was attractive; she had a pleasantly oval face and trim figure that made her look a bit like a former cheerleader. But in every comparison Chris made in that half second, Cassidy outshone Amelia in every way, right down to the shake of her shoulders.

"Well, I didn't see another car out front." Amelia grinned. "Did you walk down here, Mr. Davis?"

"Nope, parked across the street." Chris stood up out of habit. If a lady came in, gentlemen stood up. Simple as programming

—if A, then B. "Didn't want to occupy a spot needed for a customer."

"Oh, that's no problem … Chris," Cassidy said, smiling a little at using his first name. "Now, Amelia, Chris here had a good idea for iced coffee; you mind?"

"Did you make it or your brothers?" Amelia asked, and Cassidy grinned. "Okay, but keep it black for me. I'm trying to trim down."

"Why?" Cassidy asked. "You're practically a fashion model as it is!"

Amelia blushed but shook her head. "So says the former Miss Saint Cloud. Don't worry, I'll eat a good lunch later on."

"Okay, I'll be right back then." Cassidy disappeared to the back.

Amelia sat down, and Chris mirrored the gesture, even though his eyes followed Cassidy. Amelia noticed. "Gorgeous, isn't she?"

"Stunning," Chris said honestly. "No offense, Ms. Hernandez."

"We're not at City Hall; I'm just Amelia." Amelia chuckled. "And I'm not offended. So what do you think of this place?"

"It's got a lot of history," Chris said. "I don't think there's any building back home in Colorado that quite measures up, not until you get to Durango or such."

"This B&B used to be the only hotel in town, back when the stagecoaches ran through here," Amelia said. "Lots of famous people have stayed here."

"Like who?"

"Tom Landry stayed here for a vacation back in the seventies," Cassidy said, bringing out two more glasses of iced coffee, "which in these parts pretty much is like having the Pope or a president come by."

Chris laughed. Cassidy dropped him a playful wink, and left. Chris once again felt his eyes drawn to Cassidy, and he had to admit to himself that the sight of those jeans disappearing out of the room left him with some ungentlemanly thoughts.

"So," Amelia said, pulling him back to the conversation at hand, "your family ... your company."

"Yes?" Chris asked. "I hope you don't mind us moving to town, Amelia."

"Heck no!" Amelia said, surprised. She laughed, shaking her head. "Sorry, I guess I was being obtuse at City Hall. No, Chris, what I wanted to talk about was just where your family might look at establishing your business headquarters. Do you have a spot in mind?"

"There haven't been any direct discussions yet," Chris admitted, sipping his coffee. "Like I told the mayor, Andrew's the business operations guy. I just come up with the stories, and I'm able to do some light code monkeying. Sorry, industry term."

"No problem," Amelia said. "Look, I'll be direct with you, Chris. Saint Cloud's a small city, but until recently it's been a tale of two cities. In the northern parts of town, you had the Ranch Country. The folks who were 'good people' lived near what we now call Northside or around downtown. They had money. The southern arc of town was your smallholder farmers before it became Wine Country. But here, Dusty

Bend? It was 'that neighborhood,' the place where people like my parents could get a house. You understand?"

Chris nodded, pursing his lips tightly. "Is it still that way?"

"No, for the most part," Amelia said. "I mean, there's still a divide between neighborhoods, but that's on economics nowadays. I think the wineries really helped break some of those old systems. But Dusty Bend itself still … Look, you're a polite guy, but look at this place. Cassidy and her brothers could use about twice the number of customers they're getting. Now, I get it if you want to use all that land you've got on the Cloud 9, build yourself a technology campus that'll rival anything between El Paso and Austin. But Dusty Bend could use that business investment. Your HQ here in Dusty Bend would bring people coming down here. The economic impact for this neighborhood would be immeasurable."

"I can bet," Chris said, "but I know Andrew was thinking of something more self-contained."

"I won't fault you for it, but could you at least mention it to your brother?" Amelia said. "I'd appreciate that."

"I'll go one better," Chris said. "I was telling Cassidy that my brothers will be arriving next week. So how about you put together your best sales pitch, or maybe stump speech. You're a good politician, I take it?"

"Well, I've only done two campaigns, but I'm hoping I'm learning."

Chris chuckled. "I'm sure. But you do that, and I promise that Andrew will sit down with you face to face."

"Great," Amelia said. "Truth is, Dusty Bend's gotten a bit gentrified in the past few years. But to keep this neighborhood vital, it needs more than a few Latinx art galleries or an eatery or two. We need those too, but you get my point."

"I do."

"And just between us, Kim Johnson can talk all she wants about keeping Saint Cloud the way it is," Amelia said, "but the people who say that are the people who already have things the way they like it. What about the rest of us, the people who could use the tree shaken up a little bit, you know? A bunch of tech heads coming into town could be quite a good thing for Saint Cloud. Especially my district."

Chris considered the option, not ignoring the alluded to tension between Amelia and Kimberly Johnson. It wasn't his place to bite, though; that was Andrew or Brian's bag. He just wanted to tell his stories.

"I promise Andrew will listen, and my brother's a fair man," Chris said. "Thank you for the coffee. If you don't mind, let me pay?"

"Cassidy won't charge me for this," Amelia said quietly, "but if you want to leave a tip, just tuck it under your glass. She won't be able to say no then."

Chris nodded, matching Amelia's ten-dollar tip. He didn't want to show off. But he understood where Amelia came from. So, after she left the room, he quickly swiped her ten away and tucked a twenty under Amelia's glass before going out onto the porch. Noise from around the corner caught his attention, and he walked around the side, surprised to find Cassidy changed out of her blouse, wearing a plain T-shirt as she sanded a rocking chair.

"You're doing all of these?" he asked, and Cassidy stopped, turning and brushing a lock of raven's wing hair out of her flawless face. Even a touch of dust and sweat couldn't mar her face in his eyes, and when she shrugged, her smile was more genuine.

"My brothers are doing other work, and it's my turn," she said. "You and Amelia have a good chat?"

"I think so," Chris admitted. "So she's pretty new as a politician?"

"If you mean getting elected, she is," Cassidy replied. "But she cares about her district, and people in general. Want my opinion? She's the sort of politician that we need more of and who shouldn't be a politician at all. She's just too good of a person for that kind of muck."

"Didn't think there was that much politics in town."

Cassidy chuckled. "Well, we don't make the news, but like any small town, we've got our tempests in our teapots. But you can take Amelia at her word."

"Good." Chris cleared his throat. "Look, Cassidy, I, uh … I know we just met and talked for a few minutes. But I'm taking a chance here and wondering if you'd like to maybe get a coffee together ourselves. Or better yet, some tacos or something?"

"You're asking me out?" Cassidy asked, and Chris nodded. "I don't know, Chris. No offense, but I'm usually bustin' my tail here six days a week, and it's not the kind of job that clocks in from nine to five."

Chris smiled and squatted down next to her. "Writing video games isn't your typical nine-to-five either. We computer nerds can be a strange group."

"You don't look like your typical computer nerd," Cassidy said, and Chris swore that the temperature just jumped up a few degrees.

"And you don't look like your typical B&B owner," Chris returned. "So what do you say? I'd be happy just sitting out here some afternoon and having an iced coffee with you in these rockers."

Cassidy laughed. "Sure. If I can get these things finished. Which I won't do if I'm talking with you, no matter if you're a typical computer nerd or not."

Chris chuckled. "Point taken. But who knows, it might go faster than you hoped."

Chris stood up, his mind swirling with ideas. "It was a pleasure, Cassidy. I'll see you around. Soon, I hope."

CHAPTER 4

The next day dawned surprisingly cool, with a light foggy mist that felt refreshing as it permeated the air. Cassidy took relief in it, knowing that soon enough, the mist would burn off into clingy humidity. She only hoped that humidity would fade as the day wore on to be replaced with a drier Texas warmth.

"You sure you don't need help?" Carl asked her as he washed up the last of the breakfast dishes. Technically, it was his and Tim's day off, and he and Tim were planning on going out to one of the wineries to indulge in their part-time job, part-time hobby ... rabbit hunting. They were a menace to the vineyards, and it was almost a standing invitation from half of them to help control the population.

Besides, rabbit was good and could be made into fancy sausages for the guests at the B&B. That was Cassidy's one rule about letting her little brothers go shoot things, that the rabbit be put to good use.

"I'm good." Cassidy patted Carl on the shoulder. When he winced, she raised an eyebrow. "That bad this morning, huh?"

"I'll be fine," Carl assured her. "Took a couple of Advil, and walking will help it."

"Be careful, okay?" Cassidy replied. "You don't have to come back with meat, you know."

Carl grunted softly, making Cassidy smile. He didn't show it to most people, but Carl had a sense of humor, and his caveman grunting was just an example of it.

"You ready, Carl?" Tim called from the doorway, sticking his head in. "Just got off the phone with Bob Woodbury. He says we can come on out."

"Well, then, I guess we should go." Carl gave his sister a kiss on the temple. "You take it easy today, okay? And if you need us, we'll come back."

"Actually," Tim glanced toward the front door, "I don't think that'll be a problem. Come on, Carl."

Cassidy curiously followed her brothers out to the front porch, where she was surprised to find a visitor. Chris sat on the porch railing, his long legs stretched out in front of him, his hands planted wide for balance. He looked so different from the day before, the freshly cleaned and perfect jeans and button-down shirt traded in for an older, work-worn pair and an old Colorado State University Computer Science T-shirt, faded in places and with a bit of the writing peeling off. "Good morning."

"Good morning," Cassidy replied, wondering what was going on. Not only was Chris, the handsome stranger from the day before, here, but he was cute and attractive in a very different way. When he'd come by for coffee, he had a sort of "aw shucks" innocent nerdiness to him despite his fit body and lanky casualness. He looked like a nerdy country boy then. He looked like someone who would make hearts flutter on the dude ranch before going back to the office.

Now he looked right at home in Saint Cloud, a man who could put in nine hours doing manual labor and still be ready to go dancing that night. He looked totally unlike the multi-millionaire that Cassidy had figured out he was after doing a quick Google search using the information he'd given her the day before.

"Y'all play nice," Tim said, his voice casual but with a thread of steel in the undertone for Chris's benefit. Of course Cassidy had told her brothers about yesterday's visitor. She knew Tim trusted her. But trusting his sister and trusting this out-of-town new guy were two different things.

Chris watched Tim and Carl leave before turning back to Cassidy, who hadn't moved yet. "So … how're you doing this morning?"

"Confused. I thought I turned you down yesterday."

"Oh, you did." Chris chuckled, pushing off the railing and stretching out to his full height. "But I thought about it. You said your problem is you don't have enough time off, not that you didn't think I was deserving of a coffee. So I came to kill two birds with one stone."

"What do you mean?" Cassidy asked, and Chris pointed. She followed his look, a little smile breaking out on her face when she saw the big, working man's Thermos sitting at the corner of the porch, along with a tool bag. "What did you do?"

"The Thermos is mine; I got it filled up with some fancy stuff they had for sale downtown. Apologies there." Chris strode over to the bag, his worker's boots clomping on the wooden slats of the porch. "The bag I borrowed from the contractors we've got out at the ranch. They said they didn't need this stuff today."

Chris opened the bag and pulled out an orbital hand sander, the palm-sized type that Cassidy knew would make her job a lot, lot faster. "Chris …"

"Nope, no *Chris*." He smiled even as he cut off her protest. "I plan on sanding something today, Cassidy, with or without your permission. I'd just rather that I used this baby on your rocking chairs instead of on the side panels of my truck."

Cassidy considered his offer, and his stubborn obstinance. It was both gentlemanly and demanding at the same time and, in a certain way, utterly charming. She found herself grinning despite her misgivings. "Well there, smart guy, you forgot a couple of things. One, I'm not dressed to sand the chairs yet. I have to get my work shirt on."

"A smart idea; that blouse looks far too fine on you to get roughed up with sawdust and paint," Chris said, his eyes, for the first time that Cassidy noticed, tracing her body. She bit her lip. It had been a long time since a man looked at her like that, and she liked that Chris was at least taking a quick glance.

"Second, unless that's some magic tool bag there, you don't have an extension cord to get that sander plugged in," she continued, laughing softly when Chris literally face-palmed. "Forgot that bit, didn't you?"

"What can I say? Last time I used one of these was back home in the family garage. Do you need me to go get one?"

"No, no, we've got one in the pantry," Cassidy said. "Let me get it after I change shirts. And I'll bring some cups for the coffee."

"Much appreciated." Chris put the sander away and headed around the side of the house. Cassidy came back out a few minutes later, also carrying with her the can of white paint and brush she was going to use today. Chris noticed, nodding. "Division of labor?"

"Well, I got those other two finished yesterday; I don't see a reason to let the wood sit out in the elements," she said, smiling when Chris poured her a cup of coffee. "Thanks."

"You're welcome." He chuckled. "So you Texans really don't say things like 'much obliged,' huh?"

"Not all of us," Cassidy said with a smirk. "Just those of us with home training. What about you, Chris? You do pretty well with your manners."

"My mother would be overjoyed to hear you say that." Chris plugged in the sander. It was a high-end model, barely making any noise at all as he gave it a test run. "If you don't mind me asking ... your folks? You seem to be mama to your brothers."

"We're all we've got now," Cassidy said. "Mama died during the twins' senior year in high school. I was in junior college over in Abilene and would have come home, except Daddy told me if I did he was locking me out of the house unless I had my diploma with me. So I finished up school."

Chris chuckled, nodding. "Sounds like Mom. Our father died when Andrew was a freshman in college, and she went *ballistic* on him when he came home saying that he would drop out. The ear chewing she gave him convinced all of us that we were going to college no matter what."

Cassidy nodded in understanding. "Well, I'd been back about a year and a bit when Daddy had his stroke. You ask me, he just didn't want to go on without Mama, even though he tried for Tim, Carl, and me. He hung on for a while, he really did. But when the second stroke came, I think he was ready to let go. And so for the past few years it's been just the three of us."

Chris pulled one of the other chairs over and started scraping it down. "I'm sorry to hear that."

"It hurts sometimes, but that's life," Cassidy said as she got the paint can open and stirred the contents. "You still have your mama?"

"Mom's doing well." Chris smiled. "She doesn't realize it yet, but I think she's at the beginning of a relationship. She met the man at church, and I understand he's a widower, originally from Denver. He has two grown daughters. We'll see if this goes anywhere."

Cassidy laughed, humming the old Braddy bunch theme song. "Y'all are okay with that?"

"It's not our choice," Chris said. "Mom's a grown woman, and a great one at that. Besides, I know Dad would have wanted her to be happy after what happened. I don't see a problem with her having a boyfriend, and he's a good guy. I'm happy for her."

They got to work, and Cassidy felt a comfortable silence descend. The only sounds on the porch were the birds on the phone line out front, the sound of Chris scraping down the chairs, and the occasional clink when Cassidy's paintbrush tapped on the edge of the paint can.

It was the strangest first date she'd ever had, but it felt good. She didn't feel like she had to tell Chris about the mountain of debt that had come with the B&B, how their meager savings had been eaten up by Daddy's post-stroke care, or any of that.

She had a feeling he already knew.

Chris set his scraper aside and picked up the sander, replacing the sound of the scraper with the quiet hum of the sander. His arm swept over the rocker with firm, sure strokes, and Cassidy could see the muscles flex along his upper arm as he did.

"So how's the Cloud 9 coming along?" Cassidy asked. "If you're going to be here helping me, I've got to have something to fend off the gossip hounds with or else they're going to eat me alive with their innuendo."

"You can tell them that I'm not that kind of man, and the ranch is coming along well. The main house is mostly solid. The bedrooms and plumbing are already finished. And if we need to take our meals on the back porch instead of the dining room, well, that's not too much of a problem now, is it?"

"Not in Saint Cloud," Cassidy said, "as long as that porch is screened in. If not, some of the summer flies will carry off your plate before you can get a chance to take three bites."

Chris laughed. "Yeah, we'll get that taken care of. It's screened, but it's an old screen."

They kept going, time slipping away in their comfortable silence and work. Cassidy watched Chris out of the corner of her eye, liking what she saw. He worked hard, not shirking from sweat and getting his hands dirty, and making sure his work was precise and finished on each rocker before moving on to the next.

He wasn't a classic cowboy, despite the jeans and long, lean body. His boots weren't right, and she doubted any of the ranch hands around Saint Cloud would be caught dead wearing a college T-shirt. Especially one dealing with computer science.

"So your brothers help you out a lot?" Chris asked as he brought over the third chair he'd gotten stripped. At the rate they were going, Cassidy thought they'd get all of them done by the end of the day, much faster than she'd planned.

She'd have time for a date then, and she knew it.

"They're good guys," Cassidy answered, even if she wasn't quite ready to trust Chris with all of her family's information just yet. "I wouldn't be able to keep things going without them."

A truck pulled past, and Cassidy chuckled at the timing as her two brothers got out, Tim leaning on the hood of the truck as Carl came around from the other side. "Well, y'all have been productive."

"Never doubt a computer game guy with a mission. You have a good hunt?"

"Enough that we'll be eating some for a while." Carl leaned on the back of the truck. "You ever eat rabbit?"

"And a few other things," Chris said. "I mean, being from Colorado, we're famous for our Rocky Mountain oysters."

Tim laughed, and even Cassidy had to snicker. "You haven't!"

"No, but Carl there believed me." Chris chuckled. "Elk and venison are about the most exotic I've gotten. But I wouldn't be opposed to some rabbit."

"You could stay for dinner," Tim said, but Chris shook his head. "No?"

"Sorry, but about the only way you can stand me right now is that we're all outside." Chris made the guys laugh. Cassidy sniffed, and while she was still a few feet away, she didn't think she smelled anything out of the ordinary. In fact, she suspected that if she did get a whiff of Chris's smell, he'd smell like sawdust and clean, honest sweat.

He'd smell like a man, and a good one at that.

But her brothers just nodded, Tim giving a little smirk. "I understand. Cassie's very strict about us washing behind our ears before dinner."

"As she should, or else we'd be even worse," Chris said, making everyone laugh again. "You want help with the rabbits?"

"Nah, we already did the butchering out there," Carl said. "We keep the meat, the dogs get the scraps, and what's left goes in the fertilizer pile."

"Thought you weren't supposed to do that?"

Carl shook his head. "That's just if you don't want to deal with the smell. The winery keeps their compost pile far out away from the house, and it's good for the grapes."

Chris nodded, accepting the information. It was exactly what her brothers wanted to see, and while they didn't say anything, she could read their eyes. They weren't a hundred percent sold, but they were giving conditional approval to Chris as they carried the big cooler Cassidy was sure was at least half full of rabbit meat into the back of the house, where the old hand-cranked sausage grinder was ready to go.

Chris watched them before turning back around. "So, think we can get that last chair done?"

Cassidy laughed, and by working through the lunch hour, they soon had all of the chairs lined up and drying in the afternoon air. Cassidy was sweaty but felt accomplished, and Chris shared every moment with her, taking the time to wrap up his tools before getting the broom and sweeping the sawdust away carefully.

"Thank you," Cassidy said as Chris picked up his tool bag and put it on the railing. "You saved me a lot of work."

"Enough time for a dinner out?" Chris asked. "Not that I'd turn down some rabbit stew."

"Actually, it's usually rabbit sausage, and Tim makes a pretty good rabbit sausage sandwich." Cassidy hooked her thumbs in her belt loops and looked him over. "Let me ask you, Chris Davis, what are your intentions for asking me out?"

Chris chuckled and mirrored her pose. "I'm a single man in a new town, who thinks you're an interesting and very pretty woman. I'd like to spend some time with you, see if this attraction I feel between us is real or not. And while I'd be happy to keep doing chores around the house with you, I thought you deserved a classic dinner date. Fancy or casual, that's all on you."

"Well, I know Saint Cloud," Cassidy said, "and while we've got some good places to grab some food, I really doubt there's a place here that'd fit a billionaire's definition of fancy."

"Not a billionaire," Chris corrected her gently. "The company's worth a billion. I share that with Simon, my brothers, and a few hand-picked investors."

"Betting y'all are the richest people in Saint Cloud outside of maybe Justin Logan still," Cassidy said, and Chris shrugged. It was the right answer; he wasn't ashamed of his money even if he wasn't going to make a big deal about it. "Okay then, Chris Davis. We can have that dinner out. You got an idea where you want to go?"

"Nope," Chris said, "but I figure you said you don't take too many days off, and today your brothers took time off. So I've got at least twenty-four hours to figure it out. Close enough?"

Cassidy laughed. "Actually, let's make it Thursday night. I always work weekends, customers and all. And that'll give Tim and Carl a chance to get their act together."

Chris nodded but didn't move. Cassidy tilted her head, curious. "Yes?"

"Gonna need your phone number," Chris said with a smile. "Unless you just want me showing up some random time Thursday night?"

Cassidy laughed. He was cute and funny. "Sure. Get your phone out, and we'll exchange numbers."

CHAPTER 5

Black tie or blue tie?

Chris couldn't tell as he held each tie in front of his neck. He was trying to decide which was better for his date with Cassidy. The black tie was definitely a better tie, a silk one that he'd gotten eight months prior when he and his brothers had been invited to the Tokyo Game Show. In fact, he'd bought it in Tokyo, after realizing that, in all of his preparations and packing, he'd forgotten as simple yet important an accessory as a tie.

On the other hand, the blue tie was brighter, less serious and funeral-like. Tonight was supposed to be something casual, but Chris also wanted to make the right impression. So instead of a full suit and tie, he was going to go with jeans and a sport coat … with a tie.

He was the kind of man who'd never be caught dead in a sport coat with a polo shirt.

He was still undecided when he heard a truck approach the big house. He put the ties down on his bed and looked out the window, curious as to who it could be. The workers had already left for the day, and the mailman had come by hours ago. It wasn't like anyone would just casually wander down the quarter-mile-long dirt driveway that started under a huge wrought-iron archway that read "Cloud 9 Ranch."

"Who's that?" he wondered aloud as he spotted the large black SUV that was spewing dust behind it. He squinted, and when the SUV got closer, a grin broke out on his face as he saw the plates.

Hurrying downstairs, he emerged onto the porch just as the SUV came to a halt and three of the doors opened, and out stepped a trio of surprises.

"Wow, Chris, you're looking the proper cowboy!" his eldest brother Andrew greeted him. An inch taller than Chris, Andrew sported the same dark hair as Chris, with just a hint of premature gray at the edges of his sideburns that Chris suspected Andrew encouraged because it made him look more mature, wiser.

After all, when one became the CEO of a billion-dollar company in their thirties, one had to make sure people paid attention. Chris didn't care; in the creative side of the business, no one cared about age.

"What do you mean?" Chris asked, looking down at his shirt and jeans. "This isn't cowboy."

"Right," his other brother Brian said. Brian definitely didn't look the part of the country boy he was at heart, his fashionable basketball shoes and shorts looking somehow out of place in the driveway. "What do you think, Simon?"

Simon, his best friend and the other beating heart of the company, ran a hand over his freshly shaved head, smirking. "Looks like he's been eating his steaks and packing on some muscle already. What have you been doing down here, Chris?"

"Man, you …" Chris shook his head before exchanging hugs with all three of the men. "You weren't supposed to be here until Monday!"

"Yeah, well, this guy here." Brian clapped Andrew on the shoulder. "He got nervous. Kept saying that he'd come down here to find you surrounded by a disaster area and the locals ready to shoot us."

"Did not!" Andrew protested with a laugh. "The negotiations with the comic book company went faster than I expected, that's all."

"And he wanted to get down here so fast he practically laid rubber the whole way down," Simon added, grinning. "So how's life?"

"Life is … good," Chris admitted. "I made our hellos, the workers are on point … sort of getting my face known around town."

"Getting known already, huh?" Simon asked. "Well, I'll admit I'm sort of looking forward to reacquainting myself with Saint Cloud. You boys may be happy sharing this big ol' ranch house and property, but me? If we set our campus here, I'm not sure I want to live here as well. I could possibly get my own castle here in town."

"You know," Chris said, "you could check out Dusty Bend. The council member for that area, Amelia Hernandez, she really gave a sales pitch for the neighborhood."

Simon laughed, shaking his head. "Maybe, but maybe not. I remember Amelia, she's a crusader at heart. We used to call her D-a-w-n Quixote, the way she'd go tilting at windmills. Not me, I was not on her radar, but you know what I mean. Very pretty, though, if I remember?"

Chris could hear Simon's probing question, and he laughed, maybe a little nervously. "Yes, she's pretty, but not my type."

Simon shrugged it off easily. "But yeah, the Bend's a lot better than it was when I was a little kid … but I'd need to put eyes on it myself to see what sort of changes occurred."

"Amelia said it used to be the … well, not so good side of town," Chris shook his head. "I don't get it. Looked pretty decent to me."

"Well, you ask me, if I don't stay here, what I'd like to find is a few acres and a place of my own down in Wine Country," Simon said. "Don't know, though. Way the vineyards were blowing up last time I was around, the domains could be more expensive than this old ranch … Anyway, I will spend a few days in one of the spare bedrooms while I look around and make up my mind."

"Dude, that's totally fine." Chris tried to hurry things along. He knew time was slipping away and wanted to get freed up. "So I guess you want to chill out some, there's—"

"Whoa, whoa, whoa." Brian grinned. "Andrew, you see what I see? Hair all nicely combed, freshly washed and shaved even though it's six in the evening … and is that *cologne* I smell?"

"I do detect a little hint of something." Andrew smirked. "What's her name, little brother? And is she why you just so casually dismissed telling us about the pretty city council member you've gotten to meet?"

Chris felt the heat creeping up his neck; he'd never been able to hide anything from his brothers. After their father died, Andrew and then Brian both took over the older male mentorship role for the family and knew Chris inside and out.

"Whoever it is, I'm not surprised," Simon said. "Saint Cloud's got a really high percentage of pretty ladies. Maybe it's the water or something."

"And you're just telling us this now?" Brian said with a mock-shocked gasp. "If I'd known that, I'd have volunteered to come down here weeks ago!"

"And we'd already be getting run out of town," Chris joked. "A thousand broken hearts bearing torches and pitchforks would be heading for the ranch right now."

"Enough deflection, who is it?" Andrew said. "You spill it, and I'll drag these two off to leave you in peace as we go explore the ranch. That pond looks nice after two days on the road."

Chris looked over his shoulder, where he did agree, the five-acre body of water that took up a large portion of the backyard portion of the ranch house area. "Haven't explored it yet, but I plan on it soon enough."

"So?"

Chris took a deep breath and nodded. "Okay, okay ... Her name's Cassidy Norton. Her family owns a B&B in Dusty Bend."

"The Nortons?" Simon shivered. "Stories I could tell about them, the Norton twins mostly. I remember the place, historic building sort of place. Her family still owns it?"

"Well, she does technically," Chris said. "Her father died a few years back."

Simon clucked his tongue sadly. "Sorry to hear that. Still … Cassidy, huh?"

"Should I be jealous?" Brian asked Simon, and Simon nodded. "How jealous?"

"As in Chris here has a date with a former beauty queen." Simon held his hands up when Andrew gave him a withering look. "Fine. We can talk behind his back later."

"Actually, guys, about that," Chris said. "Um … I'd planned on bringing Cassidy out here. You know, a nice dinner? I stopped by the market, and—"

"And relax," Andrew said, still being the good big brother. "Chris, way I look at it, this is one big darn ranch. Plenty of room for privacy. So how about this? You go get ready, go pick this woman up. Bring her here, but instead of the dining room or whatever, you have a quiet, nice picnic by the lake? Leave the setup to the three of us."

"You mean it?" Chris asked, and Andrew nodded. Chris cleared his throat. "Thanks, Andrew."

"Hey, it's for us too," Andrew reminded Chris with a smirk. "Once we see Cassidy, I can spend the rest of the night giving Brian a hard time or calling Simon a liar. Either way, fun for me."

It was just what Chris needed—a bit of a laugh after the sudden hand grenade dropped on his plans. His brothers gave him a hard time once in a while, but at the core ... well, he knew who he'd fight with, and for, in life.

"Okay, well, I decided to go light, so it's a charcuterie board, some cheeses, and a red wine."

"Red wine?" Simon joked, smirking. "You must really like her."

Chris snorted. "Why, because I went with red wine instead of white?"

"No, because I'll let you in on a secret around Saint Cloud. Most folks, you invite a girl over for dinner, she's going to expect beer and then ... well, let's just say a *lot* of Saint Cloud was conceived in the pastures and vineyards, or in the backs of pickup trucks."

"Not my style," Chris pointed out. "Okay, I need to get ready."

"Go get snazzed up," Brian said, smirking. "We'll take care of it all. If anyone in this family knows how to create a great date scene, it's me."

"Yeah ... and we'll make sure you won't want to drown him in the lake afterwards," Andrew said.

CHAPTER 6

"How do I look?" Cassidy asked as she looked at herself in the old full-length mirror that used to be in one of the guest rooms before it developed a crack in the upper left corner. Now it stood in Cassidy's room, and she turned this way and that in front of it, trying to decide if she'd chosen the right dress.

Just the act of putting on a dress felt strange to her. At work she was in jeans almost all the time—they were dependable and durable, exactly the sort of clothing she needed for what she had to do around the property.

A dress was for special occasions. She hadn't worn once since Christmas, in fact, and under the skirt her legs felt bare, both thrilling and slightly scaring her. Thoughts of her bare legs led to thoughts of … carefree things.

And she hadn't even been on a first real date with Chris yet.

"You look fine," Tim observed from the doorway, leaning against the jamb with a little smirk on his face. "It's been too long since I've seen you look like this."

"Like what?" Cassidy asked, picking up her hairbrush and running the bristles through her hair a few times. She'd taken the time to really condition and style it some, not only soaking it in conditioner but curling it lightly in a few spots to create loose ringlets around her face. "I've gotten dressed up before."

"Not in a long time, but that wasn't what I meant," Tim said. "You're not just pulling on a dress to do Christmas or to go down to church. I mean, seeing you being feminine, trying to be pretty. When was the last time you really tried to make yourself look your best?"

Cassidy bit her lip and shrugged. "Don't know. But I mean, I have to put some effort in, you know?"

Tim blew a light raspberry, shaking his head. "Don't even start with that business, Cassie. You're still gorgeous, and this guy sees it. You just do a good job of hiding it behind a ton of work."

Cassidy looked around her room, shaking her head. "This place needs more."

"Yup, and for tonight that's on Carl and me," Tim reassured her. "I don't even want you thinking about work until eight o'clock tomorrow. You do, and I'm duct-taping your door closed."

Cassidy laughed softly, remembering the memory from their childhood. She'd been in her old room then, the one that was next to the linen closet, and due to a weird foible of the doorknobs, Tim had been able to tape the handles to each other, using most of a roll of duct tape before attempting to sneak out with Carl for a party.

Too bad Tim had forgotten that Cassidy's room had a huge window that allowed her to be waiting for them by the truck, her arms crossed and her eyes fiery.

Now, though, it was a good laugh between the two, and Cassidy relaxed a little. "You really think I look pretty, Tim?"

"Prettiest girl in Saint Cloud," Tim assured her. "And if this guy doesn't recognize that, then he don't deserve to take you out."

She knew her brother was just talking her up, but it helped. It helped more when she came out and saw Carl behind the front desk, wearing a fresh-pressed shirt and giving her a smile. "You look great, Cassie."

"Thank you, both of you. You sure you're going to be okay?" Cassidy asked, and Carl nodded.

"Sure of it. I'll be right here until late, and Tim's going to make dinner. Nothing fancy—grilled peanut butter, right, Tim?"

Tim groaned but nodded. "You won the coin flip; you got to pick dinner."

Before Cassidy could ask why they were flipping coins for dinner choices, the rumble of a truck came to her ears, and Cassidy hurried over to the front window. "It's him!"

"She acts like she's going on a date with Kenny Chesney," Carl quipped, and Cassidy sighed. But she kept her eyes on the truck as Chris shut it off before getting out and approaching the front door. Unable to hold back her nervous eagerness, she stepped out before he reached the porch so she could get a better view. Carl chuckled. "Have fun!"

She waved behind her head, her eyes fixed on Chris as he approached. He'd gone for the perfect blend of dressed up and casual, the dark sport coat matching with his jeans and hair and just … everything.

"You clean up well," Cassidy said as Chris looked at her, his eyes widening slightly as he got to take her in fully in the light. "What is it?"

"I know I'm still young. I know that there's a lot of the world I haven't seen," he said, his voice quavering slightly, "but I have never seen a sight as beautiful as the one before my eyes right now."

Cassidy blushed and walked down the steps of the porch carefully. "You are definitely a storyteller. Let me guess—in school you got As in English?"

"Actually, no." Chris offered her his elbow. With almost a knightly tenderness, he walked her toward his truck, a newer model four-wheel drive that looked freshly washed but was definitely a truck that had seen some work, too. "My teachers kept telling me that my writing was too fantastical. Took me until junior year of high school to realize that fantastical did not mean the same as fantastic."

Cassidy laughed. "So you turned to video games."

"Hey, in a video game, nobody questions why you've got your hero riding on a tiger that sprouts eagle's wings yet has a rocket engine underneath." Chris opened the door for Cassidy. Even though he was being a gentleman, Cassidy could still feel his eyes follow the length of her leg as he helped her up, and she smiled.

Apparently, Tim was right. She was pretty, at least in Chris's eyes. The thought warmed her as Chris came around to the driver's side of his truck and got in, cranking the engine. "I suppose I should tell you now," he said a bit nervously, "there's been a bit of a change in plans."

"Oh?" Cassidy asked, biting her lip. "We can't go to the ranch?"

"No, no ... but about a half hour before I came to pick you up, my brothers, Andrew and Brian, and my best friend, Simon, arrived," Chris said. "When they found out I was bringing a lady to the ranch, they insisted that we keep our date, but ... well, they're probably going to want to meet you. But they promised they'd give us privacy."

"Oh," Cassidy said with a soft laugh. "Okay, I thought it was something serious. Remember, I've got two brothers too. The past couple of nights, dinner's been like a very persistent interrogation."

Chris laughed. "Yeah, although Simon's from Saint Cloud, you know. He knows who your family is, so he's probably filling in my brothers on everything. Like you being a beauty queen?"

Cassidy gasped, laughing. "Why is it that nobody can let that go? It was a decade ago, and I only did it because it was a thousand-dollar scholarship for college!"

Chris laughed, and for the rest of the ride, they chatted about anything and nothing. It was casual, easy talk, discussing everything from the weather to how the rocking chairs dried. Cassidy felt at ease with Chris, even as he pulled onto the dirt ranch road that led out to the Cloud 9. "You boys are going to be cleaning your trucks down a lot in a few months with this road."

"Nah," Chris said. "I'm a firm believer in conservation. As long as it's just cosmetic, I'll leave the dust and dirt on my truck. Except for special occasions, of course."

"Well, don't count me in those occasions," Cassidy pleaded. "I don't mind a bit of dust on a truck."

Chris chuckled, and a moment later they came to the entrance to the ranch. She'd been by, of course; at some point or another she'd driven almost every road in Saint Cloud. And this was on the way out to the bigger Happy W and Bar-X ranches.

But it had been a long time since she'd gone under the big wrought-iron gateway trundling up the long driveway. She took in the big two-story ranch house. She could see the renovations still being done, the work site that was on the one side of the house, but it was still a huge, beautiful home, white with black trim and a black roof. Cassidy was surprised until she saw what made the roof black.

"Y'all are putting in solar panels," she noted, and Chris nodded. "Some folks around here are going to think you boys are a bunch of tree-hugging hippies."

Chris laughed. "Then they can pay the power bills for us. After what Amelia said, we might adjust some of our plans, but my brothers and I are on board with using as much self-produced electricity as we can."

"Smart man," Cassidy observed with a smile. "And don't pay those chuckleheads any mind. Your ranch is your ranch."

They pulled around to the back of the house, into the parking area that Cassidy was familiar with. Visitors park out front, family and friends out back. Chris got out, and as he came around, Cassidy looked at what was revealed in the sunset light.

"I see the barn and stables are still here," she said. "Originals?"

"I think so. They're both going to be renovated." Chris looked over at the two big buildings. The barn was bigger than the main house, easily the size of two basketball courts inside. The stable was smaller but still noticeable with its one side open to the air. "The mayor wants to hold dances there."

"Oh really?" Cassidy asked as her eyes cut to movement she saw in the main house. She turned her head, but before she could say anything, the two faces in the window disappeared, making her chuckle. "We're being observed."

"Then let's enjoy some privacy." Chris led her toward the large pond—or it might have been a small lake; she wasn't sure. "I haven't tried to swim here yet, but I plan to soon enough."

"Is it ... clean?" she asked nervously. "You know, there used to be cattle and horses around here."

"From what the real estate people told us, the lake wasn't used by the cattle, but I'll still have someone come out and do a water analysis," Chris said. He knew it was better to do some maintenance on ponds, something about balancing fish population, plans, algae and whatnot. Up ahead there was a soft glow, and Cassidy was charmed as she saw a small table set up on one grassy shore, along with a blanket and candles. Chris was obviously impressed as well. "Guys did good."

"It's pretty." She held Chris's hand as he helped lower her to the blanket before taking off his sport coat and settling down on the other side of the blanket. In the soft yellow glow, she felt his eyes studying her, and she searched for conversation to shift the focus off her. "So are you going to go into holding any cattle?"

"Nah. But I have reached out to the neighbors, seen how they might want to use the fields. From what I can tell, they're pretty wild. Nobody's been taking care of them for years."

"Sounds about right," Cassidy said. "What about horses? Seems a shame to live out here on this big ranch and not have a horse."

Chris laughed, reached into a basket underneath the small table resting on the blanket to take out a bottle of wine, and started unpacking the food. It was light fare, meats and cheeses mostly, along with some fancy-looking breads that complemented the whole thing.

"We'll figure something out," he said. "Wine?"

"Please," she remarked, watching as he deftly uncorked the bottle and poured a glass. "What's that mean, figure something out?"

"Well, I can ride some," Chris said, "but I'm no horse expert. I'd need to buy a horse, for sure. I was thinking maybe a pureblooded Arabian, and then the stableboy can take it out for daily rides and …"

Cassidy's lips twitched as his voice faded away, and she saw through him. "You think you're funny."

"Your lips are saying you think so too." Chris lifted his glass. "Cheers. And please, whatever looks good to you, just eat. I'm not one for fancy forks, and if this is too fancy, next time we'll stop by the A&W Stand I saw downtown, get some hotdogs and tater tots."

Cassidy laughed softly and plucked a piece of cheese from the platter. It was delicious, nutty and creamy at the same time, definitely not the kind of stuff she bought for the B&B. "So what kind of guy are you, Chris?" she asked. "How'd you grow up?"

"Like I told you, Dad passed when Andrew was in college and I was in junior high." He sighed softly as he took a sip of his wine. "We did okay, middle class, I guess you could say. Mom had a good job, and Dad's life insurance paid off the old house. I mean, we weren't rich. I still did after-school jobs and stuff like that to have spending money, but it was good for me, I think. I came to learn the value of what a pair of fancy shoes was in terms of sweat, not just dollar amounts. So when it came time to go to college, I didn't waste time. It was time to get to work."

"Which is how you were able to make a game so quickly."

Chris chuckled, nodding. "Didn't seem fast at the time. But yeah, that and Simon. We met in a freshman intro to computer science class and were best friends by the end of the semester. We roomed together the whole four years, and when we weren't studying, we were making *Sky Adventures* together. He's a … That man's a genius at coding, ten times faster than I could ever be. When his mom passed away, my family sort of adopted him, I guess you could say. I mean, he slept on our living room couch for the first holiday break, and then, afterwards, he got his own bed in my room, where we spent three summers in a row, the two of us coding for ten to twelve hours a day."

"That doesn't sound healthy," Cassidy remarked. "And you don't strike me as the guy with a body type to stay hunched over a computer all day."

"Why, thank you, but that's what the rest of the day was for. We had it planned out. Sleep eight hours, code for ten to twelve, eat our meals next to our screens. Add in a little bit of time for showering and bodily needs, we still wedged in at least an hour a day for exercise. Jogging, bicycling, some of my father's old PT workouts from his time in the Marines."

"Your father was a Marine?" Cassidy asked, and Chris nodded. "Career?"

"Nah, only four years to pay for his college," Chris said. "But he taught us some of his old routines, the playing card workout, the dice workout, just going crazy with pushups and situps and pullups. Honestly, I think he did it because he had four boys who had too much energy and needed a way to get it out of us." He cleared his throat and wiped at his eye. "Sorry. Sometimes it still hurts, you know?"

"I know," Cassidy said. "I still cook biscuits the way Mama taught me as a little girl, but half the time Carl can't finish his because it reminds him of Mama too much."

Chris took a deep breath, nodding. "Anyway, part of it's also that after we got *Sky* released and we knew how successful it could be, I started working saner hours and actually signed up for a regular gym. Nothing fancy, or I guess you could say fancy in that it had all this cool stuff, but it wasn't some poofy place."

"I know the type of place," Cassidy said. "Here in Saint Cloud, you've got very few options. There's one of those women's only fitness places over near Northside, there's the high schools for the kids, the YMCA, and there's one CrossFit psycho out in Dusty Bend."

"No yoga studios?"

Cassidy chuckled. "You want yoga in Saint Cloud, you can go to the YMCA, First Methodist Church, or you can go to another town." After Chris laughed, she looked at him more evenly. "So what are your long-term plans, Chris Davis?"

"Personal ones?" he asked, and she nodded. "Well, while I do know computer coding, I really like telling stories. That's why I first did with Simon, and while the game gets edited, storylines tweaked to fit the market, all of that … I'd like to use our new venture, Cloud 9 Games, to make the world a better place."

"Cloud 9 Games?"

Chris nodded. "*Sky Adventures* is a joint project. When we got started, we had to partner with someone to fund it all. But Andrew's promised me that the next game, it's going to be all us. So we were thinking, why not Cloud 9 Games?"

It made sense to Cassidy. Moreover, it told her that whatever else the Davis brothers were doing, they were planning on sticking around Saint Cloud for the long term. It reassured her and allowed her to think and look at Chris in a whole new light. No longer was he just a handsome stranger, a new guy in town who might disappear over the horizon in a week or a month.

He was someone she could look at spending time with. And with his unique mix of brains and brawn, good humor and quiet, hard-working demeanor, he was looking even tastier than the cheese and wine. Taking a sip of her drink, she smiled. "Can I admit I'm a little jealous?" she said. "You've got these big dreams. I've known my entire life that I was going to probably take over the B&B. Especially when Carl had to give up football."

"What happened?" Chris asked. "I mean, they look like football players."

"They were, until Carl tore his ankle to pieces," Cassidy said. "Tim stayed in school, but Carl … he was in a dark place. Got pretty deep into the bottle at the time. And with Daddy the way he was, I had to take care of him. I pulled him up, and I'm proud of that and who Carl's become, but … well, let's just say having the options you've got makes me a little jealous."

Chris nodded, not contradicting her, which she liked. Most men would have fed her a bit of fluff about how she didn't have to limit herself or downplay their luck. Chris did neither; didn't make any promises he couldn't keep.

After the food was gone, the sun had fully set, only to be replaced with a big, three-quarters-full Texas moon. It wasn't as bright as it'd be in a week, but it was more than enough light to see by when Chris stood up and offered Cassidy a hand. "Would you like to walk?"

"I think I can do that." She took his hand. They started off, and as they walked, Cassidy was thrilled as Chris didn't let go of her left hand. Instead, he held her hand in a strong but gentle grip as they walked along the shore, helping steady her when her shoes threatened to betray her.

"Are you planning on sharing that house with your brothers forever?" Cassidy asked, and Chris chuckled.

"No. I mean, I might stay here on the ranch, but eventually I figure we'll start … needing independent family spaces. Young couples need privacy, I heard."

Cassidy laughed. "Good point."

Chris didn't press the issue, which surprised her a little bit. Even the most respectful of boys she'd dated when she was younger would have made at least a slightly risqué quip. Then again, Chris was different from any of the guys she'd ever dated before.

They completed their walk, and Chris led her back to his truck. Tension filled the cab of the truck as she anticipated his move. There was always a move, from her first date back when she'd been fifteen all the way to her last date over a year ago.

Some of them had been smooth, or cute, or something that made her go along with it to a certain point. She had already kissed a guy on the first date, although she'd never let anyone past the proverbial second base until much later.

Chris had been so sweet, so interesting, so … perfect that for him, she was seriously pondering relaxing that rule. But as he drove, he kept his eyes on the road, his hands firmly upon the steering wheel until he pulled up outside the B&B.

Here it is, Cassidy thought as Chris shut off the engine. *He's going to make his move. What am I—*

She never got a chance to answer that question as Chris got out of the truck and came around, opening the door for her. In an almost strange mirror of him picking her up, he offered her his elbow and walked her politely up to the front door of the B&B before stopping.

"I had a wonderful evening." Chris stepped back, taking Cassidy's hands. "Thank you for coming to the ranch."

"I had fun too," Cassidy said. He was only a few inches away from her, and she could feel the warmth of his presence and the reaction of her body as her heart sped up in anticipation. *Okay, here it comes!*

But it didn't. Instead Chris gave her hands a little squeeze before stepping back, bowing before turning away from her to walk quickly back to his truck and climb inside. She was so stunned at the sudden change she didn't even know how to react, saying nothing until his cherry taillights disappeared down the street.

Her heart was still pounding, and her body was saying it wanted something she hadn't felt in a very long time.

So where was the guy who was going to give her what she wanted?

And why had he left without so much as a goodnight kiss? She'd given all the signals, she thought.

Did he not like her? Did she do something wrong?

What was going on?

CHAPTER 7

"So the contractors could divide up the work crews," Andrew said as he, Chris, Simon, and Brian gathered on the porch early the next morning. After last night, Chris felt like he still needed about an extra three or four hours of sleep. He'd tossed and turned half of the night, his body wishing he'd done things differently on his date.

That and Brian, who had chosen the bedroom next to his, snored like a Harley-Davidson chainsaw. That was unusual, and Chris suspected his brother had a bit of an allergy to something in Saint Cloud. Either way, Brian already said he was heading into town to get checked out by a doctor, so that was a bit of good news.

"So you're considering the mayor's request to hold events in the barn?" Chris asked Andrew, who nodded.

"Yes. In fact, while Brian's seeing the doc, I'm going to go say hello to the mayor myself," Andrew said. "But first thing's first, I'm going to go meet with one of the neighbors. I've got a morning coffee arranged with Amanda Munoz. Maybe we can get the horse situation straightened out. You and Simon are okay to keep an eye on things around the ranch, right?"

"Sure," Chris said. "Actually, if you don't mind, while you're out, stop by the agricultural supply place on Schneider Avenue. I saw a Honda sign there when I drove by. I think that while having some horses would be nice, having a quad runner or some other kind of ATV would be good too. Easier on the suspension for our trucks, at least."

"Smart idea," Andrew said. "Sure, we'll stop by. I wanted to do some grocery shopping and get some things for the house anyway."

After watching Brian and Andrew drive off in the SUV, Chris and Simon got to work. Their first stop was the old barn, which was mostly empty but could use some cleaning before the crews got to do their renovation.

"This harrow's too old for most farms," Simon said as they looked at the rusty old piece of spiked farm equipment, "but you know, if you want, you could do a little bit of artistic renovation to this thing, sort of use it as an art piece. There'd be some folks around here who'd like that sort of nostalgia kick."

"Suppose we could hook it up to the truck, haul it out into the space between the barn and the stable."

Simon shook his head. "It's light enough, man. Between the two of us, we could get it out of here ourselves. Just grab a handful of that drag chain."

Chris agreed, and between the two of them, they managed to get the harrow out of the barn. It was a lot easier than Chris thought it would be, at least until they hit the outside dirt and the hook-like sprinkles started digging in a little. "What would they use this for, anyway?"

"I'm no farmer," Simon grunted. "But I think this is how you condition the fields. I think some farmers use it to spread fertilizer and manure."

"And are you full of manure?" Chris joked, making Simon laugh. They got the device out and to a good spot and dropped the chain. "I suppose that's good enough. You know what you want to do to, what'd you say, turn this into art?"

"Probably first we'll just go to town on this thing with some wire brushes, get that sort of lightly rusted look." Simon shrugged. "Either way, better out here than letting the contractors haul it off."

"Good point."

Simon and Chris went back into the barn, looking around at the wooden walls and the floor. Again, Chris was struck with the idea that the bones of the barn were still strong. It just needed a little bit of work. He'd been having that thought a lot around Saint Cloud. "How does it feel?" he asked Simon, who was looking at some of the old hand tools that were still in the corner. "Being back in town?"

"I barely slept last night. I just couldn't wrap my brain around the fact that I'm here again. Last time I came back was to bury Mom, and now… I know I talked you guys into coming here, but strangely, it doesn't quite feel like home."

"Yet," Chris said encouragingly, grabbing some of the old tools to carry them out to where the harrow waited. "We really need to get another dumpster out here for this stuff."

"Eh, just dump the garbage in the back of your truck, and we can throw it into the dumpster at the house," Simon said. It was a good idea, and Chris turned right to his truck, where he dropped the rusty tools.

"So aren't there people who buy this junk?" he asked. "I mean, if we're doing the harrow …"

"Might help to reach out to some of the antiques stores in town," Simon said. "You know, there's some in Dusty Bend. Like a certain date of yours."

Chris chuckled and looked over at his friend. "And?"

"And you didn't tell any of us a single peep when you got back after dropping her off," Simon said.

"You know, kissing and telling isn't the right thing to do. What are we, a church Bible study?" Chris asked, and Simon laughed.

"No, we're worse," Simon said. "Now I know you well enough, and I know you weren't gone long enough after you two left to take her home to say you did anything scandalous. So you can tell me a bit, right?"

"It was a good date," Chris finally said. "I was planning on calling her this afternoon, try and set something else up."

Simon probed some more, but Chris wasn't answering anything else about Cassidy Norton. Instead the two spent the next hour clearing out junk from the barn, sweating through their shirts before the first of the work crews showed up to take over the task.

"We'll drop this by the dumpster," Chris told the work crew leader before he and Simon drove back over to the house, emptying the back of his truck before pausing to take a drink. With the men hard at work on the house, the whole area was noisy, and Chris felt like there wasn't really any place he wasn't either getting assaulted with noise or getting under foot. "Hey Simon, you want to head into town?"

"You sure?" Simon asked as he drained the last of the lemonade in his glass. "Andrew and Brian already headed in."

"And? I'll text him. Things are fine here, and the work crews know their jobs," Chris pointed out. "You can show me more of town than what I've seen. I think I've barely scratched the surface of town."

It was more than that, but Chris didn't say it. He heard the nervousness, the pain in his friend's voice. He knew that Simon was second-guessing his decision to come back to Saint Cloud, and while there was no way he'd try and force Simon to stay if he decided he hated it here, he wanted him to give the town a fair shake.

"Okay, okay." Simon caught the keys when Chris tossed them his way. "Seriously?"

"You know where to go, not me."

They started off, Chris texting Andrew before they left. The only reply he got was that he needed to be back by noon, which was fine with Chris. As they headed toward town, the radio softly played the only FM option—country music, of course. Chris didn't mind. While he preferred rock to country, he'd grown up in an area where country was ubiquitous. And KCLD didn't go too far into the twangy depths that he knew country could be.

"So first I'll take you by my old house." Simon turned right and headed toward the Rio Plata. "We were practically on the river."

"Sounds nice," Chris said, and Simon shook his head. "No?"

"Nah. I mean, I get where you're going, house on the river and all that, but you've got to see the Plata. It's not like we were backed up against some awesome waterway or something. The area I lived, the river isn't even deep enough to fish in most of the time. Although I do remember floating down the river on an inner tube when I was kid, which was pretty sweet."

They pulled up in front of a plain white house, the front lawn patchy in areas and an older-model Ford Ranger pickup parked out front. Simon pulled over, looking. "Looks like they redid the trim," he observed. "Lawn needs work, though."

"Maybe they're saving money on water, you know how it is around here."

Simon nodded. "You know, growing up in this house, there were times … times I didn't quite understand what my mother went through. Why she never told me about how I came about."

"Was there anything in her effects after she passed?" Chris asked quietly.

He knew the stories, of course. Pattie Smith had been a woman on whom fate hadn't smiled. While Simon never quite said it outright, Chris suspected at various times that Pattie had some mental health issues that never quite got fully treated. He had never asked Simon about it. Could a child think that about their mother, especially when they're the only parent?

"No." Simon put the truck back into gear and pulled away. "Anyway, this is a pretty decent neighborhood. About the closest thing you'll find to the suburbs here in Saint Cloud. Bland, but overall a good place to be a kid. We could ride our bikes through the streets, play ball in the park, and … that's where we need to go."

Simon hung a left turn, driving through downtown to the western edge of downtown and Dusty Bend, where a huge monolith appeared. Chris had heard about places like this before, of course, and had seen larger in his life.

Still, it felt weird to pull up outside a football stadium that was legitimately the largest building he'd seen in Saint Cloud. It probably didn't have the square footage of the high school that was across the street, but it certainly rose much, much higher into the air. "Wow."

"Municipal Stadium." Simon shut off the engine and chuckled. "Come on, let me show you the beating heart of Saint Cloud for most of the year. Gates are always open; messing with this place is like peeing in a church pew."

They walked through the gates, Simon leading Chris up the aluminum stairs that emerged into the middle of the huge stadium. It was mostly metal, row after row of aluminum bleachers that ringed the entire field, which was the sort of deep yet bright green that told Chris it was an artificial surface.

"The stadium was different when I was a little kid," Simon said as they climbed higher, walking up the steps toward the press box that afforded them a little bit of shade. "Back then, Muni was totally different, a Depression-era hulk of concrete with a few bleachers on the ends by the end zones. But this is Texas."

"Where football is second only to church, and that's up for debate," Chris said, and Simon snorted, nodding. They took seats, looking down over the field. Chris had spent his fair share of time on fields the same dimensions, but as he looked out over the huge stadium, the lines that were permanently a part of the artificial turf, and the running track that surrounded it, he had to whistle. "How many people does this place seat?"

"Ten thousand four hundred and ninety," Simon immediately rattled off, laughing softly. "That's before you add in the standing-room space along the fence or near the snack shacks over there in the corner. I've seen over fifteen thousand people packed into this place for the Civil War games."

"Civil War?" Chris asked, then nodded as he remembered his first conversations with the mayor and Kim Johnson. "The local rivalry."

"Saint Cloud High and Schneider High." Simon chuckled and shook his head. As if on cue, a group of boys in shorts, cleats, and fitted undershirts emerged from a large building in the corner of the stadium complex and jogged onto the field, one of them carrying a bag full of footballs. They were all lean, obviously serious about their football.

"Summertime practice?" Chris asked, and Simon nodded. "Really?"

"Trust me, they'll be out here every day," Simon said. "I remember doing the same thing. All those hours in the sun, sweating my tail off … you know, looking back, it helped."

"How so?"

"You don't ask. Your brothers don't either, and I thank you for that," Simon said, "but I was an angry kid. Single parent, barely getting by, on the free lunch program at a school where most of the kids didn't ... I went to Saint Cloud, by the way. Anyway, football let me release that anger; taught me a lot about discipline too."

"Focus, which is why you're such a good code monkey."

Simon laughed. "Yup, guess I am. By the way, you're in a bit of a pickle now. You're going to need to pick a side in the Civil War."

"How so?" Chris asked. "It's local high schools. You know we had some serious football in Colorado too. Lots of folks bleed orange and blue, green and gold, or black and gold."

"What, no Air Force blue and white?" Simon asked, laughing at Chris's gesture of a reply. "Yeah, well, that's small potatoes. Meanwhile you just happen to live right in the middle of Saint Cloud territory but had a date last night with the sister of two of the biggest terrors Schneider High ever produced."

"Tim and Carl?" Chris asked, and Simon shivered. "That bad?"

"They were younger than me, so I missed when they really, really filled out," Simon said, "but those two ... they lived up to the Schneider mascot, the Red Devils. Those two were demons on the field. They played both ways at times, but mostly on defense. Tim was an outside linebacker, Carl a free safety, which really meant another linebacker around here. The hits they laid out were the stuff of legend, man. Everyone figured they were a lock for the NFL ... until Carl screwed up his leg."

"What happened?" Chris asked. "I get the impression it was bad; Cassidy said something about his ankle."

"I don't know everything," Simon said, "I mostly heard it second and third hand. You sure you don't want to ask Cassidy about it personally? Or Carl or Tim?"

"Figure I should know the terrain a bit before I get really in there," Chris said. "It'd help."

Simon thought about it for a moment and nodded. "Okay, I get that. Well, both of the Nortons got scholarships to D-1 schools, although separate ones. Heck, maybe that's what hurt Carl in the end. He and Tim both decided to graduate high school ASAP so they could enroll quick, get that first college spring ball in. Tim did fine, and while the local estimates of him becoming an NFL star were a bit overblown, he did go on to be a two-year starter. Guess he did okay."

"But Carl didn't."

"Carl got hurt in the first spring practice sessions, messed up his leg something fierce," Simon said. "Dunno what, but whatever it was, it more or less ended his football career. Or at least took him out for a year. During that time he found the comfort of the bottle."

Chris winced. "Ruins more people than anything else."

"For Carl Norton, it put him on a dark path. What I heard since then, well … look, let's just say I heard some whispers when I was back to bury my mom. But it's nothing for certain. Eventually he got kicked out of college. What I can tell you is that you need to watch yourself."

"Why's that?" Chris asked as he watched the players on the field run pass routes. "Nice catch down there."

Simon looked, squinting. "Can't be sure, but that looks like one of the Munoz kids. Could be wrong, but anyway. For you, you gotta understand … off the field, the Nortons were okay guys. It wasn't like the A&W was a battleground if SCHS players and the Nortons were there at the same time. But on the field, angry? They were mean and nasty, and I heard whispers that Carl's trip to the dark side has kept him that way. So I gotta ask you, you want to be part of that drama?"

Chris considered and nodded. "I want to date Cassidy, not Carl."

Simon laughed. "Not the way things work in Saint Cloud. Now if you want to know how to survive this, I got a price."

"A price, huh?"

"Yup," Simon said. "You have to give me at least a few details. Seriously, man, Cassidy Norton was like every high school boy's crush. So?"

"So I took her home, walked her to her door," Chris said. "I was a gentleman."

"Dude, come on!" Simon shoved his shoulder. "You can at least tell me if it was a good kiss or not."

"Kiss?" Chris chuckled. "I don't know. I suppose she's a good kisser, but I didn't try for one."

"What?" Simon asked, shocked. "Why not? Did she give you the no signal? Did you not want one? No, you're crazy, but not *that* crazy."

"Yes, I wanted to, and I think she was giving me the signal, but no, I didn't try for one," Chris said. "I've got my reasons."

Simon nodded, propping his elbows on his knees as they watched the football players below. "Yeah well, you might have messed up, buddy. Look, Saint Cloud girls might not be big city freaks, but ending a good date without even a goodnight kiss? You're playing with fire."

Chris nodded and watched the football players. "I'll be careful." Down below, the players kept going, sweating in the late spring sun, and he thought about Simon's warnings. Finally, he cleared his throat. "So what else is there in this town?"

Simon thought for a moment and chuckled. "Want to know where you might be able to take Cassidy on a second date? Then we can head back to the ranch?"

"Wouldn't mind."

Simon stood up. "Then follow me."

CHAPTER 8

"Cassie."

Cassidy didn't hear her name, just kept wiping at the windows with the old piece of newspaper, getting the last of the streaks out of the glass. But her mind was anywhere but on the glass in room 7.

What was that the night before? Sure, it had been a little bit since she'd had a first date, but she wasn't that far out of the loop.

She knew how things went. Boy meets girl, boy and girl spend time together, at first in groups but then in private. It's called a date.

And if things go well on that date, they end the night with a kiss. Some girls would go further; some girls would go all the way. That wasn't Cassidy, but she wasn't ignorant. She knew the truth of the world.

While she'd had a few dates that didn't end with a kiss, those dates were final dates, bad dates. They were the dates with guys she didn't want to see again anyway.

Chris Davis hadn't been that way. Every moment out at the Cloud 9 had been a good one. The cold cuts, or whatever fancy name they wanted to give the pieces of meat, had been delicious. The wine even more so.

But it wasn't the food that made her date with Chris a good one. Instead, it was Chris himself. The way he'd listened, the way he responded to her comments. Even in the way he held her hand as they'd walked along the shore of the lake, not feeling the need to fill every moment with mindless chatter. Chris Davis was a man full of stories, but that didn't mean he had to blab on constantly.

So why had he just turned and walked away at the end of their date? Was he not interested in her? Was that why he'd just dropped her off politely without even a single kiss?

If so, it hurt. She hadn't had a good date end without a kiss in a very long time.

"Cassie … Cassie!"

Cassidy blinked and turned around to see her brother standing on the other side of the bed, his face slightly pale as he tugged a pillowcase up and over one of the three pillows meant for the bed. The rest of the bed, however, was half made, only two corners tucked in on the fitted sheet, and the main sheet itself still folded on the nightstand.

But Cassidy could see the issue. It was the pain in her brother's eyes. Setting her wad of newspaper down, she turned away from the glass. "Bad?"

"It's been better," Carl admitted. "Just, could you maybe get that side of the sheets?"

"No problem." She tugged the sheet smooth and pulled the fitted sheet over the corner of the mattress. "Sit down, Carl. You know there's no way to control when your ankle's going to be good and when it won't be."

"Stupid docs," Carl grumbled, limping over to the chair on the side of the room and slumping down. He didn't want to; his pride kept him on his feet a lot longer than he really needed to be. And Cassidy suspected that, somewhere in the world, there was a doctor who could fix her brother's ankle. Or maybe a therapist, or someone.

Whoever it was, they certainly weren't on staff at the university when Carl got injured. It wasn't even a "real" football play—she'd seen the video. The team was running a non-contact drill, and he was covering a receiver when their feet got tangled up. An awkward step, a two-hundred-and-thirty-pound body rolling over his leg, and two botched surgeries later, Carl's football career was over.

Either way, after what happened when Carl started drinking, his reputation was sealed. People in Saint Cloud saw Carl as broken, and every time he let any sort of pain show, people mistook him for being drunk again, or angry, or whatever.

The truth was her brother was just in indescribable pain, and after how he got thrown out of college, he refused to drink, he refused pills any stronger than a Tylenol. He just ... dealt with it.

"So after this room, I want you downstairs, soaking your ankle in the bucket," Cassidy said. "No complaining, or else I make you get in the big clawfoot tub."

Carl shivered and shook his head. "Fine, fine. Don't do much good, but it makes you happy."

Cassidy smirked, knowing her brother was full of it. He just hated admitting weakness. "The other day, I was looking at something on my phone. I know it's not anything new, but I was thinking you might want to start doing those alphabet ankle rehab things again."

"You realize how stupid I look with an overgrown rubber band around my big toe, writing the alphabet in the air?" Carl growled. When Cassidy didn't flinch, he sighed. "Fine. *If* you tell me why you're all sorts of messed up after your date."

"What do you mean?"

"I mean, you cleaned that same pane of glass four times, and your face keeps shifting from confused to angry to just ... not all here," Carl said. "What went down?"

Cassidy sighed and nodded. If anything, it'd get Carl into the bucket and doing his ankle rehab. "The date was fine. He took me out to his ranch, where I sort of met two of his brothers."

"Sort of?" Carl asked, and Cassidy nodded.

"They spied on us through a window from about fifty feet away or so when we parked his truck," Cassidy said. "It was kind of funny, like something you and Tim would do."

"Probably."

"Then we had a picnic on the edge of this small lake that's part of their ranch. It was nice, candlelight and cheese, some meat, funky breads," Cassidy said with a soft chuckle. "Nothing too crazy. I'm sure you could find all of it down at the corner store, but it was nice. After that we walked along the shore, and he brought me home."

Carl tilted his head. "So what's the problem?"

"The problem is … he dropped me off without even a kiss on the cheek!" Cassidy admitted. "I'm just, did he not like me? Did he not want to kiss me for a reason? Carl, I know it's silly, but I feel like a woman who's withering on the vine here in this B&B. Sixty, seventy-hour weeks, I feel like I'm having my youth *sucked* out of me by this stupid building, and I don't know what I can do about it!"

Her voice had risen, almost to a yell, and Carl looked at Cassidy in shock. "Cassie—"

"Chris is a handsome, smart, even sexy man," Cassidy said miserably. "He's what Mama would have called a 'good catch.' And I just … To think I can't even get a man like that to kiss me at the end of a date … sort of sucks."

Cassidy was venting, not really meaning a hundred percent of what came out of her mouth. She was frustrated more than anything else. So when Carl jumped to his feet, his eyes blazing, she was caught off guard, so surprised she took a few steps backward until her butt rattled against the dresser. "Carl?"

"Nobody disrespects my sister," Carl growled before turning and moving out of the room a lot faster than anyone in his amount of pain should have been able to move. Cassidy tried to follow him, but Carl in a mood was a machine, a man who could ignore all sorts of pain in order to do what he wanted to do. By the time she got downstairs, he was already out the door and in the B&B truck, pulling away in a rattle of pebbles that had her covering her eyes.

"What the heck is up with him?" Tim asked, coming out onto the porch. "I was in the kitchen working on that clog in the drain when I heard the front door slam and ... what?"

"I think Carl might be in a mood." Cassidy reached for her pocket and pulled out the phone. "I sort of vented about my frustrations with last night's date, and he stormed out."

"Frustrations?" Tim asked, and Cassidy waved him off. "Cassie?"

"Nothing to get in a twist over. I was going to handle it myself with a phone call after our work was done, but now we've got a situation." Knowing her brother the way she did, Cassidy called Chris first to try and warn him off. But almost immediately the phone went to voicemail, and Cassidy growled. "Crap."

"What?"

"He's not picking up," Cassidy said. "His phone must be off or something. Which means ..."

"You don't want Carl to catch that boy unawares." Tim stuffed his hands in his pockets and continued with tenseness in his voice. "I dunno if he can fight or not, but we know Carl can. So it's either he whoops on Chris Davis, or Chris and his brothers whoop on him. Either way—"

"I know." Cassidy went into the phone's contact list and flipped through the names there. "Hey, did you take the rifles out of the truck from your hunting trip?"

"Of course. Locked up in the safe," Tim said. "Carl ain't that type anyway."

"Yeah." Cassidy found the right name and hit dial. She hadn't used the number in a long time, but she'd kept it around just in case for situations like this. She didn't want to get him involved, but she didn't have another car or truck, and he could do something.

"Hello?" a deep voice answered, and Cassidy felt her stomach quiver a little. "What's going on, Ms. Norton?"

"Sheriff Monk, it's Carl," Cassidy said tersely, ignoring Tim's reaction to her calling the county sheriff. "I think he's in a mood to lay a beating on someone, and I'd like to avoid blood if we can."

CHAPTER 9

Getting back to the ranch, Chris and Simon were just in time for a bit of a surprise as Amanda Munoz herself pulled up to the ranch house, a horse trailer behind her big truck.

"This is a bit of a surprise, Ms. Munoz." Chris walked toward the truck. "I guess Andrew had a good visit?"

Amanda Munoz climbed out of the truck, adjusting her cowboy hat as she did. A sturdy woman in her late forties, her long ponytail was streaked with silver, but her stride was still as strong as someone half her age. Three more people got out, and with a gesture of her hand, they went around to the back of the trailer while Amanda approached Chris, offering her hand. "Your brother's a man who knows what he wants and doesn't fluff around," Amanda said with a chuckle. "Good to see you again, Chris."

"Thank you, Ms. Munoz," Chris said, shaking it. "So he bought some horses?"

"Two this time, but he said once your brother Dylan arrives, you and him get to pick out your own," Amanda said. "So we'll get these two stabled up, get the tack put away, make sure you're ready for another delivery. Andrew said the stable needs some TLC but is strong?"

"I wouldn't put a Kentucky Derby racer in there. The stalls need a good leveling and some fresh hay, but we'll get that taken care of," Chris said. "Thank you for this."

"Well, I've got a couple of geldings that are ready to be saddle trained, so I've got a few extras on my hands." Amanda walked with Chris around to the back of the trailer, where one of the hands was unloading a beautiful chestnut bay horse with a star-shaped burst of white on its nose. "This here's Nova. He's a five-year-old gelding. A good boy, he's strong and steady, just right for riding in the pasture land. He'll take you on a trot for hours, but be careful with galloping him. He's from a line that's got a knee issue, and I wouldn't push him if you don't need to."

"Is that why you've gelded him?" Chris asked, and Amanda nodded.

"Too many breeders look at the performance of a horse from only one perspective." Amanda walked up and patted Nova's nose. "I get it. They want a horse that's stronger, faster, springier. But there's something to be said for a good horse that stays healthy for fifteen or twenty years. It's not fair to Nova, I guess, but I had to nip his line in the bud … literally."

"Well, he'll have a good home here," Chris assured her, carefully approaching Nova on his left side and reaching out to rub his muzzle. "Hey there, buddy. So who's going to be your rider?"

"Andrew picked him out, and this baby was Brian's choice," Amanda said as her hands brought out a beautiful golden palomino. "She's a mare, but Brian didn't care. He saw that coat and that was it."

Chris laughed softly. "Yeah, Brian's a bit of a showboat. What's her name?"

"Jasmine," Amanda said. "She's seven, and a strong bloodline, so if you ever want to breed her, she's a good choice. Come on, let's get them walked down while my men drive the truck down to get the rest of the stuff unloaded. Your brother drives a hard bargain."

Chris chuckled. He could hear the respect in Amanda's voice at her declaration. He hadn't had a lot of time in Saint Cloud, but he'd heard that nobody was a shrewder businessperson than Amanda Munoz, who didn't let anyone's stereotypes of what kind of person should own a ranch deter her from running the best dude ranch in the state of Texas.

"So what sort of bargain did he strike anyway?" Chris asked. "Hopefully, it wasn't too stiff."

"No, it was tough but fair," Amanda said. "The Happy W will get a nice long strip of acreage along your northern side to drive our dude tours through, almost doubling the length of our tour land and letting us not have to use the government land up north as much. In return, y'all get Nova and Jazzy."

"Literally horse-trading."

Amanda chuckled. "Suppose so. The equipment he's paying me a fair price for, and the next two horses will be cash, but that's just a delayed trade too, really. I'll be giving him that money back next January to pay for the rent for your acreage."

Chris nodded; it sounded like Andrew. Taking one of the lead ropes, he walked with Amanda down to the stables, where her three workers were already unloading stall mats and other materials from the back of the truck. Chris noticed that all of them were handsome in a classic cowboy way. "You hire good workers."

Amanda chuckled, hearing his unspoken question. "Helps with the tourists. They're not just eye candy, though. I don't hire that kind of worker. Male or female."

"You have female hands at the Happy W?"

Amanda nodded. "Including my own daughter."

"Cool."

They got to the stable, and Chris clipped Jasmine's lead off on one of the iron rings that were mounted to the posts on the open-air side of the stable, laughing when Jasmine promptly did what horses were best for. "Is that an endorsement of your new home, Jasmine, or a condemnation?"

"It's a reminder that horses require work," Amanda said matter-of-factly as she clipped Nova to a ring of his own. "You ready for it?"

"We'll take good care of them," Chris assured Amanda. "Although I'll admit we might be talking your ear off with questions. I know how to ride, and the basics. I'm no horse expert."

"Not a problem," Amanda said. "Horses are like babies. You take care of the basics, give them lots of love, and you've solved seventy-five percent of your issues. Now, if I can offer you an expert tip. Horses are also like relationships … you need clear communication to make them work."

Chris looked over at Amanda, who lifted an eyebrow. "What have you heard?"

"Just that you've been seen at the Norton's," Amanda said, "and that you're no handyman. Now, I'm not saying it's a huge issue, but if a man comes around to sand my rocker, I'm thinking things. Catch my drift?"

"You've got good ears."

A truck roared into the backyard, causing Chris and Amanda to look up. Chris identified the truck—it was the Norton's—but was surprised when Carl was the one who got out. Amanda identified him as well. "And you've got to learn about Saint Cloud."

"Davis!" Carl bellowed, his voice ringing out clear through the air. "Chris Davis! Get out here, boy, you and I have some talkin' to do!"

"I suggest you keep your hands up when you talk," Amanda said. Chris nodded, heading toward the truck. Carl was clearly enraged, and he didn't want to have a possible fight around the new horses.

Amanda was probably thinking the same thing since she said, "I'll keep my boys and the horses here."

Carl saw Chris before he was halfway across the yard, his face turning pink as he started toward Chris. He was limping slightly, but that didn't seem to slow him down as he came at Chris like the former football player he was. Chris had barely opened his mouth to ask what was going on when Carl's big hand, a work-toughened hand that was also big enough to palm a football with, crashed into the side of Chris's face, sending him tumbling to the dirt.

"Get up, boy," Carl growled, his fists balling up. "Nobody disrespects my sister!"

Chris realized that Carl's first blow had been little more than a slap, and wondered just what he'd stumbled into. It felt like a sledgehammer had exploded against his cheek.

But the pain faded as he got to his feet, anger and adrenaline numbing his cheek. He might not have been a real cowboy, just an ersatz one who spent most of his twenties working in computers, but Chris Davis was nobody's boy.

Chris brought his hands up, and Carl threw again, a looping right hand that would have caved in the side of Chris's face. Except that Carl didn't know something about Chris. Back in Colorado, he'd learned to box after a junior high school bully had made his life miserable. With Andrew and Brian in high school, Chris had to defend himself, and he did. Sure, the Police Athletic League lessons weren't going to make him a professional, but they were still there, kept sharp through the years by bouts on a heavy bag whenever life's stress got in the way.

So it was with some satisfaction that Chris felt Carl's hand go whistling past his ear just as he crashed a fist into Carl's rock-hard stomach. Normally it was enough to put someone down, but Carl just grunted before kneeing Chris in his thigh.

Both of them were limping now, all thoughts of form or rules forgotten as fists thumped into bodies. Carl butted Chris in the head, Chris's head snapping back as he felt blood start to flow from above his eyebrow.

Carl's lip split as Chris's hand blasted him in the teeth, his resultant grin bloody and feral. He tackled Chris again, and the two went rolling along the ground, down the slight slope that led to the lake.

"Carl!" Chris bellowed as he elbowed Carl in the back, trying to get to his feet again. They were on the sandy shore now, and Chris could feel the grit already stinging the cut above his eyebrow. Carl rolled away, and they got back up again. He was woozy; Carl's tackles were harder than his punches, and Chris's ribs felt like they were caving in. Breathing was hard, and as he jabbed at Carl's face, there was little in it.

Carl took the blow directly on his nose, grinning through it as he hurled himself at Chris again. This time it wasn't just a tackle; instead, he lifted Chris into the air, his arms wrapped around Chris's waist as he drove the two of them into the lake, both of them splashing under the shallow water, sputtering as they both came up.

Or at least Chris did. Carl slipped, groaning in pain and dropping to a knee as his ankle gave way, and Chris pulled his punch before he could hit the helpless man. "What is this about, Carl?" he panted as he slogged backward a few steps. He stayed in the water, however, figuring that if Carl wanted to go all NFL on him again, the water would at least slow him down some. "Disrespecting Cassidy?"

"Yeah, you disrespected my sister!" Carl panted, groaning as he gingerly got up. "Took her out, wined her, dined her … and then you didn't even give her a goodnight kiss? What the hell's wrong with you, you stupid or something?"

Chris sputtered and dropped to his butt in the shallow water, laughing. "That's what this is about?"

"Yeah!" Carl said.

"By *not* pressing an advantage, I disrespected your sister?" Chris laughed. "You know most brothers go on a rampage after a guy *takes* advantage of their sisters?"

Carl sputtered, then started laughing. Within moments the two sat in the bathtub-deep water, laughing their heads off as Amanda and her men approached carefully. They were joined a few moments later by Simon, who had with him a tall, slightly paunchy man in a brown uniform with tan pants, a Sam Browne belt across his torso, and a Smokey the Bear hat on his head.

"Well, I guess it looks like we've settled things," the tall man said. "What do you say, Amanda?"

"Looks like the two boys slipped and fell in the lake, Sheriff," she said. "Don't think your services are required."

"No, but since it's my first trip out here in a long time, might as well make myself useful," he said. "You boys need to go to the hospital or anything? You've picked up a pretty nasty gash over your eyebrow there, Mr. … Davis?"

"Yeah, and no, I'm good." Chris struggled to his feet. He offered a hand to Carl, who took it and let Chris help him up before the two of them struggled from the lake, Chris supporting Carl and his bad ankle until they got to the shore. "Sheriff Monk, I assume?"

"You assume correctly." The sheriff offered a hand. "Steve Monk. And you're Chris Davis."

"One of probably a million in the USA." Chris shook his hand. "What brings you by?"

"Heard I might need to mediate a tussle," Sheriff Monk said. "Miss Norton said there was a misunderstanding. Seems you two worked it out?"

"More or less," Carl said. "But I got a question that still ain't been answered. Why'd you *not* try to kiss my sister?"

Chris looked around, seeing that there were six other people interested in his answer, and shook his head. "No disrespect, Carl, but that's a matter between me and Cassidy. Now, I was planning on calling her tonight and asking her about another date, but …"

He reached into the back pocket of his jeans and pulled out his phone, which dripped with water and was bent in two places. Carl blinked and turned pink. "Dang."

"Here." Simon pulled his phone out. "I can share phones with Chris for a day or two."

"I don't have a phone," Carl said, "but I'll write the number down. Y'all got a scrap of paper?"

"Inside," Chris said. "We've got a first-aid kit too."

Carl chuckled and nodded. "Sounds like a good idea. We should get that eye of yours patched up if you want to take Cassie out."

The two men turned toward the house, seemingly close friends, and Chris heard the chuckles from the others. He knew the story of the fight would be all over town by the end of the night, but he didn't care. He wanted to smooth things over with Cassidy as soon as possible.

Well, that and get Carl patched up. He apparently had enough to worry about without sending her little brother back to her with a busted lip and a few other injuries.

"Say," Chris asked as they mounted the steps to the house, "how's the ankle?"

"Just a pinched nerve, you wanna know the truth," Carl said. "Dumb docs messed up my surgery. I'll tell you about it while we get patched."

"Sounds good."

Outside, Chris could hear Simon and the sheriff chatting. "You think they're okay?"

"Yeah," the sheriff said. "Don't know your friend there, but Carl's an okay sort. Just don't make him angry; people don't like him when he's angry."

"Clearly."

———

"Hey, Mom," Chris picked up the call on the first ring on his new phone. "I'm acclimating and learning the local customs."

"That's not what I heard," Marianne Davis chuckled; she loved teasing her sons.

"Um?"

That wasn't the answer she expected. "The word is that you're getting yourself into all sorts of trouble. You sure pick a strange way to make new friends."

"Who's the rat? Which one of my brothers told you about Cassidy?"

Now that was interesting. Andrew had told her about a tumble in the lake with a local young man but nothing about a Cassidy.

"Who cares? You know you can't hide anything from your mother."

"I know, Mom, but …"

"So you like this girl?"

"I do, but we've just met, so don't start printing the wedding invitations just yet."

Marianne laughed. "Okay, I won't, but I expect you to let me know as soon as you decide it's time for me to come and meet this Cassidy."

"I promise, Mom."

"In the meantime, I wanted to ask—how's Simon doing?"

"Simon?" Chris seemed surprised by her question.

"Yeah, how is he adjusting? I'm sure it can't be easy for him. Is he happy to be back?"

"I'm not sure. Some days he's real excited, and some days he's second-guessing his decision to come back here."

"I'm sure he'll find his marks eventually," Marianne said.

They chatted for a few minutes before Chris announced he had to run.

Marianne put her phone down and looked thoughtfully at the big envelope on her desk.

"Oh well," she said, talking to herself. "I've waited so long already, I can give Simon another month to settle before turning his world upside down."

CHAPTER 10

"You look pretty tonight."

Cassidy didn't acknowledge her brother, still too upset over what had happened two nights ago, having her little brother get escorted home by the sheriff, showing up on her front door still filthy with mud, a split lip, and bruised ribs.

And according to Sheriff Monk, Chris had gotten the worst of it too!

How was she supposed to date a guy—how was she supposed to have a *life*—when her brother went off battering guys like that over a single date?

"Cassie?"

"Carl." Cassidy turned away from the mirror and put her lipstick down. "You know I'm still mad at you, right?"

Carl stuck his hands in his pockets, looking like the world's biggest four-year-old, chagrined. "I know. I'm sorry, Cassie. I'll say it a thousand more times if I have to."

Cassidy shook her head and took a deep breath. "Your heart was in the right place, you doofus." She crossed the room to hug her brother. "I know you wanted to defend me. But, I'm a grown woman, Carl. And you can't go off like that."

"I know, I just … okay." Carl hugged Cassidy back. "At least I learned one thing about that man."

"What's that?"

"He might be a computer nerd, but he *definitely* does not hit like a computer nerd," Carl said with a lopsided grin, made all the more lopsided by his still split lip. "Man can throw a good shot."

"Ugh, you're a caveman, you know that?" Cassidy rolled her eyes and shoved Carl away a little. "By the way, you know I'm going to punish you for sticking your nose in my affairs, right?"

"Right," Carl said uncertainly. "How?"

Cassidy marched across the room to her dresser drawer, opening the top drawer and taking out the long, thin loop of latex rubber and handing it to Carl. "Fifteen minutes a day. *Every* day."

Carl looked like he was about to argue for a moment but instead took a deep breath and nodded. Sitting down in the wooden chair next to Cassidy's door, he pulled off his boot and sock to loop the resistance band around his big toe before pulling back with his hand on his hip. "A … B … C …"

"Fifteen minutes, Carl. Not a second less," Cassidy said, going back over to finish her makeup. "And by the way, thank you for saying I look pretty."

She felt pretty, too. While the jeans were something she'd wear on a daily basis, this particular pair was her special jeans, the ones that hugged her hips and thighs a little bit more, maybe a bit sexier than she'd wear for work. And the sleeveless black top she was wearing was *definitely* not work wear. It wasn't tight enough to show off every one of her curves, but it did show that while she might not have been Miss Teen Saint Cloud any longer, she still had a waistline and figure that could at least get her top ten at the Mrs. Central Texas pageant if she'd wanted to enter.

"Well." Carl softly grunted, keeping his toe writing in the air, "I think you hit just want you wanted to go for."

"And what's that?" Cassidy asked. "And who made you a women's fashion expert?"

"Nobody but my own two eyes," Carl said, "and you're going for pretty but not cheap. Am I right?"

Cassidy chuckled and put her makeup down to pull on her boots. "You know, Carl, if you ever show another woman this amount of insight, you'd probably score yourself a keeper."

"Maybe," Carl grumbled as he finished the first round of his ankle exercises and lowered his foot to count in his head to thirty before starting again. "But then who'd keep Tim in check when he goes and does something foolish?"

Cassidy laughed and finished getting ready. Right at five o'clock, early for a normal date but not for what Chris said he had planned, he pulled up out front, getting out of his truck and meeting Cassidy on the porch. "Cassidy."

She tilted her head, feeling butterflies in her stomach. He was also wearing jeans and boots, although his were lace-up work boots. He'd put on a white cotton shirt, a nice one that gleamed in the afternoon sun and made his broad shoulders look even broader. His eye was still a swollen mess, and Cassidy noted the butterfly bandages on the gash over his eyebrow, wondering who'd done it for him. It was a decent job, and she'd patched up a few wounds herself over the years.

"Chris. How's the eye?"

Chris smiled a little, shrugging. "I can see out of it, and it'll go down. Besides, your brother told me something while we were patching ourselves up."

Cassidy chuckled. "Let me guess. *Pain heals. Chicks dig scars. Glory lasts forever.*"

Chris laughed. "Yup."

Cassidy shook her head. "Men and their football movies. Come on."

Chris walked her to the truck, just like last time, and again was a total gentleman as he helped her in. On the way to the ranch they chatted, mostly about their days.

"The renovations are coming on quick. Andrew's got something twisting in his head, and he doesn't want any distractions when he's ready to drop it on us," Chris told her as they passed through downtown. "I figure he'll wait until Dylan and Matt Miller arrive to tell us, but it won't be long now."

"Matt Miller?" Cassidy asked, and Chris nodded.

"He's Dylan's best friend. Sort of like Simon and I, except Dylan's got a family of his own. But he asked if he could come hang out for at least the summer, maybe see if he could help out with the company. Of course we're not going to turn down the help; if anything, we'll put him to work around the ranch."

"You Davis boys collect up strays like magnets," Cassidy said with a small laugh. "Sure you don't want to run for town dog catcher?"

Chris laughed. "I'm sure. What'd Sheriff Monk do if we did that? I noticed the other day he didn't wear a gun."

"Oh, Steve Monk's got a gun," Cassidy said, "but he doesn't take it out of his car unless he has to. He's sort of old-fashioned that way. Likes to talk things out, work with the community instead of act like he's at war with the community. Still, he's nobody's fool."

"How so?"

"He doesn't carry a pistol," Cassidy explained. "If he feels like he needs to carry something, he'll have a Remington shotgun in his hands. Twelve-gauge double-aught buck, or at least that's what people suspect. He's never had to fire it in the line of duty."

They got out to the ranch, and Cassidy chuckled as she saw the three men sitting on the back porch as Chris helped her out of the truck. One of them waved, and she waved back. "You think they'll ever just come out and say hello?"

"Oh, probably when we're done, they might," Chris said. "I sort of had to tell them everything after the sheriff came out."

"And you're going to tell me?" Cassidy asked, and Chris nodded. "Promise?"

"Promise ... after we've got privacy," Chris said. They walked down to the stable, where Cassidy saw two gorgeous horses, a taller chestnut one and a golden palomino that looked like every little girl's dream pony, even if it was a horse. "Say hello to Nova and Jasmine."

"They're beautiful." Cassidy smiled as Chris produced a couple of carrots from a small bag on the wall and handed her one. "Who's first?"

"Well, your choice," Chris said. "I figure we can take them both out; they're both really calm horses. Andrew did a great job picking them up from Amanda Munoz."

"The Happy W, huh?" Cassidy offered her carrot to Jasmine. "Smart choice. Not taking anything away from Justin Logan and the Bar-X, but with Amanda doing more dude ranching than real ranching, she specializes in calm, easy horses. Just like you, aren't you, Jasmine?"

The horse whickered softly, taking the carrot from Cassidy and letting her pet her muzzle. It was beautiful, and Cassidy felt like a country princess as she and Chris saddled up the horses. She felt even more like a princess when Chris brought out a surprise for her. "Thank your brother for telling me your hat size," he said as he presented the black straw cowboy hat to her. "I was lucky to find one that matches with your outfit, however."

"It's beautiful ... Thank you." She put it on her head. "How do I look?"

Chris's chin dropped, and the look in his eyes told her everything she needed to know before he could find words again. Finally, he cleared his throat. "If there is a more beautiful woman in all of Texas right now, I can only pray there's a man lucky enough to be looking at her the way I get to look at you."

"You're a silver-tongued devil … Come on, I want to hear more."

In the early evening light, Cassidy relished the feeling as they left the main house area of the ranch and headed into the fields. Cassidy wasn't the most experienced horsewoman, but she'd done enough riding in her past to be comfortable on top of Jasmine. Next to her, Chris rode on, swaying on Nova perhaps a bit more than what an experienced horseman would do but keeping good control of the horse.

"So how long has it been?" Cassidy asked. "Since you rode?"

"Consistently?" Chris asked, and she nodded. "Probably two or three years. You?"

"I probably only ever ride every six months or so," Cassidy admitted. "When I was little, my parents would take my brothers and me out to the Happy W once or twice a month for the trail ride program Tony Munoz, Amanda's father, ran. But that stopped … well, when Mama passed away."

"You're probably better than I am," Chris replied. "I'm not too proud or too stupid to know I'm no expert. If anything, I'm shocked you agreed to come up here with me."

"Why?" Cassidy asked, and Chris laughed.

"Cassidy," he said as they reached the top of a slight hill on the backside of the lake. From up here, Cassidy could see the enormity of the Cloud 9 ranch off to her left, while to her right there was the house area, the lake, barn, and stables. She felt like she was on the border of two different worlds, but both of them were in the hand of the man next to her.

"Chris," she said. "Is this private enough?"

Chris nodded. "Cassidy, the reason I didn't kiss you after our last date wasn't because I didn't want to. I ... want more."

"More," she repeated, and he nodded. "As in?"

"As in that's why I brought you up here to talk," Chris said. "About what might happen after tonight. Cassidy, since my brothers and I got rich, I've had ... well, plenty of people trying to get close based off money alone. I'll give Saint Cloud credit for that—this isn't a town that cares about money. At least, not too much."

"You need to meet more people."

Chris laughed quietly. "Probably. But from the moment we first talked there in your dining room, I could tell you didn't care."

"Well, I do happen to like how you clean up." Cassidy smiled. "That takes a bit of green."

"True, but I feel like we could take Jasmine and Nova back to the stables and have this date at the taco stand on Memorial Drive. We could sit in the stands at Muni Stadium sharing a couple of Twinkies from the gas station down the road."

Cassidy laughed. "That might be pushing it a bit. Now if you made it a big bag of Doritos, you'd be on point."

Chris smiled. "Yeah, well, I know that I'm not a real cowboy. Even if I just lived off the money my family has now, I'd never be more than a 'dude' cowboy at best."

"That's not important to me," Cassidy said. "You're sweet. You make me laugh. You work hard, even if some of that work I don't know or even understand. Your ability to ride a horse doesn't measure up to that."

"I know … which is why I want to keep seeing you, Cassidy." Chris reached out and put a hand on hers. This close, their horses were practically pressed together, and she could feel the warmth of his leg against hers along with the touch of his fingers on top of her hand. "I'd like to say we're seeing each other officially."

"If we were a few years younger, I'd say you need to talk to my parents." She smiled as she took his hand and gave it a squeeze. "Then again, I guess you got Carl's permission already."

"Yeah … your brother's got a hard head. Literally."

She laughed softly. "He'd be happy to hear that. By the way, he said you can fight a little bit. But that's not why I'm saying I'd like to keep seeing you, Chris. I don't need a man to fight for me. Nowadays that'll just get you in trouble more than anything else."

"True."

"But, Chris, what I want is to be with someone who makes me feel alive. Who makes me feel seen, and respects me, and … well, more than just the owner of a struggling bed and breakfast. You do that. When I'm with you, I feel like I can remember the dreams I used to have and not think they're so ridiculous. Which is what confused me so much at the end of our last date."

Chris nodded and took off his hat, propping it on the horn of his saddle. "Cassidy, I wanted to. I didn't because, like I said, since becoming rich, I've had too many people try to cozy up to me. Especially women. Now, the kid I was who left to go to college and was suddenly surrounded by thousands of examples of the female form? I'd have been like a kid in a candy store."

"You mean college wasn't a candy store?" Cassidy asked with a smirk, taking her own hat off and propping it on her saddle horn.

"Oh, it was, but at the time I was the broke kid in the candy store. Still snuck a few pieces, more than I should have," Chris admitted, shrugging. "I'm not proud of it. In fact, I started feeling like things had lost their meaning. Kissing became no more intimate than a high-five, and waking up next to someone was as much confusing as it was meaningful. So I made a choice when *Sky Adventures* released. I wasn't going to play that game any longer."

"And what is your game now?" Cassidy asked, her heart pounding in her chest. She thought she knew where he was going, but she had to hear the words from his lips. She had to hear it to still the bees running around and around in her head.

"I want every moment I spend with someone to mean something," Chris said. "I wanted to be a hundred percent sure, in my brain, in my heart, in my soul, that every gesture we make is one we a hundred percent mean."

"And if you kissed me now, would it mean something to you?" Cassidy asked. "Because it would mean something to me. It would have meant something last time too. I don't know about your college girls or the girls who you've met since you got rich. But I don't hand kisses out like lottery tickets."

Chris didn't chuckle or laugh, his face grave and his eyes intense as he nodded. "It would mean a lot to me."

Their eyes locked, and Cassidy could feel herself drawn closer to Chris. In the golden light of sunset, she could see the future in his eyes, and it was as good as any dream. Their heads tilted, their lips just an inch or so apart, when Jasmine whickered and pulled her away, stamping her foot on the ground.

Cassidy chuckled. "I think she wants to run."

"Amanda said I should be careful with Nova," he countered, but smiled. "But I can take him up to a trot safely."

"Well, then, how about this," she said, looking out. In the distance on the pasture land there was a tree, a beautiful oak whose branches stretched out so wide that even from half a mile or more away, it dominated the pastureland. "I'll race you to that tree. Let's see if you can have a little fun and *earn* that kiss I know you want."

Chris plucked his hat off his saddle and perched it on top of his head. "Little lady," he said in a comedic, classic cowboy drawl that had her smiling, "I do believe you're on. And you better be prepared for a memorable kiss."

Cassidy put her own hat on and nudged her forward without warning. "Come on, slowpoke!" she called over her shoulder. "You better not disappoint me!"

She was sure he wouldn't.

CHAPTER 11

Chris knocked on Andrew's home office door, holding his new phone. "Guess what? Problem solved."

Andrew looked up from his laptop, chuckling. "Now let's work on the next problem you've got. Gravity."

"What do you mean?" Chris asked, tucking his new phone away without telling Andrew that he'd already been swapping text messages with Cassidy. He felt giddy enough without it.

"I mean that ever since you got back from riding the horses with Cassidy, you've been *floating*," Andrew said with a smirk. "And the way you looked when you introduced her to us? Your mouth was practically cramping you were smiling so hard."

Chris shrugged; it was true. "And?"

"And I'm happy for you … but I need you to get your head in the game," Andrew said. "I've got a business issue I need your help with."

Chris nodded, coming fully into the office and giving Andrew an even look. "What's going on?"

"The download charts." Andrew turned his laptop around. "*Sky's* plateaued, and with the next game being at least six months to a year away, we're in danger of losing our foothold."

Chris nodded, seeing the download ranking charts. *Sky* had never been the number one download on the various app stores but had consistently been in the top ten for most of its release life. "How's the in-game purchases?"

"Still strong; we're making profit, but if this download trend continues, the market could move on before we're able to land our next product," Andrew said. "Now how's the coding department looking?"

"Truth?" Chris asked, and Andrew nodded. "If you're asking if we can speed up the development of the next game, you're dreaming. I mean, it could happen, but we'd be dropping quality and be scrambling to patch bugs left and right for three months post-release."

"Not the quality I want us to be known for," Andrew growled, and Chris nodded in agreement. His brother might not have been a computer nerd, but they could agree on one thing. They put out a quality product. "Which is why I had another idea. An update patch for *Sky Adventures*. You told me once you had storylines plotted out for years, right?"

"Right, but a lot of that I incorporated into the next game," Chris said. "We can't gut *Phantom of the Kingdom* for an online update."

"No, but I know there's stuff you cut out of *Phantom* because it didn't fit the overall narrative. Why not take some of that and make it into an update for *Sky*?" Andrew asked. "You can meld the storytelling, right?"

"Of course ... it'll be the coding that'll take the time," Chris admitted. "Even if I've got templates on the servers, that's a lot of work to do."

Andrew drummed his fingers on the desk and nodded. "What do you need?"

"What's my timeline?"

"End of the month? Six weeks?" Andrew asked, and Chris's mind started spinning. A gigabyte of updates ... four to six weeks.

Well, there was the Treasure of Argon storyline he'd considered before dropping the idea because of the name. But if they renamed it, tweaked some of the meme-worthy ideas he'd had, they could...

"I'd need a team, elite code monkeys," Chris said after a minute, fully in computer mode. "The best we've got. And I need them here. None of this telecommute garbage. I want them coding in the same room, same time collabing."

"That ... will be a challenge," Andrew said, and Chris nodded. "This house is only half done at best, and there's no way they have any work space on the ranch."

"Then we put them off the ranch," Chris said. "There's space in Saint Cloud."

Andrew nodded, tapping his chin. "I can make some calls. Look, if I can get the team into town by Monday, do you think you and Simon can ride herd on them, keep the team pounding the keyboards, and get it done in four weeks?"

"Sure. I'll need a dozen. Fifteen would be better. If someone can flash the backup server at the main offices and bring it with them, that'll make it even easier. I'll have a LAN party ready. We can beta run the update at the same time we're coding. At that point, uploading to the main server can be done in the off hours overnight, not slow us down."

Andrew held up his hand. "Too geek-speak for me. Give me numbers I can take to the RE/MAX downtown, square footage, power supply, internet needs. Maybe if we're lucky, they'll throw in a bathroom or two."

"On that … let me talk to Cassidy," Chris said. "For temporary lodging."

Andrew read his brother's mind clearly and nodded. "Okay. I'll support you on this, Chris, but be careful. You two literally just started things and are taking baby steps, it seems. Mixing business with feelings at this point is a really, really fine line to be on. Even at the best of times, it's dangerous, you know."

"I know," Chris said, "but it's worth the risk. Cassidy's B&B is struggling; I've never seen it even half-full. A solid month of booking the entire place will at least give the Nortons some breathing room. Do you mind if I talk with Cassidy about it?"

"I wouldn't see it any other way," Andrew said. "But I want to be there with you when it happens. I'm the nickel-and-dime guy, after all."

Chris took a deep breath and nodded. "You're right. So, um, with me putting in twelve-hour days coding, who's going to take care of the house and stuff?"

"Dylan and Matt will be arriving before the coder team shows up," Andrew reminded him. "I think our little brother and his freeloading friend can start helping by shoveling the horse stalls out and getting them as sweet as Cassidy's kisses."

"Hey!"

Andrew laughed. "Gotcha, little brother."

"Keep it up, Andrew," Chris growled, "and you and I will be having a discussion."

"Oh yeah?" Andrew said, grinning and bringing his hands up from behind his desk. "I'll just toss you in the lake like Carl Norton did."

Chris got to his feet, grinning but still not letting Andrew get away with it. "You got thirty seconds to get your ugly butt out in the yard before I yeet you through the window."

Andrew got to his feet as well. "Oh, it's on."

CHAPTER 12

Red.

Red.

Red.

Black.

Red.

Red.

Cassidy sighed as she looked at the balance sheet on the computer, wishing that she'd done things differently when she'd set up the accounting file. Yeah, it made sense from a certain perspective. It made the sheet easier to read, quicker to see if an entry was positive or negative.

But the sea of red that stared back at her was depressing.

Sighing, she looked at the final account balance, then clicked back a page, and then another, and another. The trend was as clear as it was perpetual.

They were going broke. If things didn't turn around within the next three months, she was going to have to make a decision. On one hand, she could sell the B&B. The property was theirs outright and could easily pay for a nice house in Dusty Bend or even one of the cuter little houses in the Northside even without throwing the business in as well.

The other option? Fire one of her brothers. The overhead for the business was actually rather small. With the property paid off, most of what she had to cover was the cost of three grown adults.

But could she fire her own family?

A knock on the doorframe caused her to lift her eyes, and she saw Tim standing in the doorway, his work gloves in his left hand and his sweat-soaked shirt sticking to his chest and abs. "Hey, lawn and trimming is done." He wiped a hand across his forehead. "What's wrong?"

"Why do you say that?" Cassidy asked, and Tim tilted his head, an expression he'd had his entire life when he was calling out his sister on her poor attempts at lies. "Fine. I was doing the accounting."

"Let me guess, a sea of red?" Tim asked, and she nodded. "If only Gordon Ramsay was still doing that show of his, what was it called, Hotel Rescues or something? I'd even fake yelling and drama if needed."

"I don't know, but I know what you mean," Cassidy replied, sighing. "But that doesn't really matter. Here, you can see for yourself."

Cassidy passed her laptop over to Tim, who sat down and went through the spreadsheets before whistling through his teeth softly. "Crap."

"Yeah. Way things are looking, unless we have a crazy busy summer, we're not going to make it through the year," Cassidy said softly. "So I'm trying to decide which way I think about going."

"Let me guess … sell or one of us leaves to get another job," Tim said, and Cassidy nodded. "Okay then, problem solved. I'll find another job."

"Tim!" Cassidy protested. "How can you—"

"Because I can," Tim said simply, without any rancor. "Cassidy, Carl still needs this place. He's getting himself together, but you know how he is when his ankle's acting up. He growls once, and half this town thinks he's going to turn green and go rampaging through downtown. Three-quarters of town won't give him a chance, and leaving Saint Cloud would be like ripping out his heart. And he needs you, not me. Me? I can do all sorts of stuff. If anything, I can probably get a job out at the Bar-X, or maybe go work down in The Depot."

Cassidy shivered at the idea of her brother working in The Depot. So named because of the cattle depot Saint Cloud's ranchers would use, it still was the home of the county fairgrounds and most of Saint Cloud's industrial connections to the rest of the country.

But it was also the most dangerous neighborhood in town, with Sheriff Monk often assigning half of his officers to cover The Depot at night. The idea of her brother working in The Depot horrified her, honestly. "Tim—"

"Cassidy, I'm not saying I'm planning on going down there now, and I'm definitely not going to truck driving school or something silly like that," Tim said. "I'm just saying that if anyone has to leave, I'm the one who should do it. I can still keep my room here, even."

Cassidy took a deep breath, feeling her stomach twist and clench. Since their parents died, they'd been together. At first they needed to, to support each other and to deal with the loss of Mama and Daddy. As the years passed, they were an imperfect family, but they were family.

To see a crack in their unity because of economics wasn't right.

"Tim, I don't want you to have to get a job, you know that. I'll… I'll figure something out. We've still got some time."

"Sure, I know that. But I'd rather have that pad there if the water heater breaks or we need a new stove." Tim held up a finger before she could answer. "Visitor."

Cassidy listened, hearing the boots coming down the hallway. And despite her emotional turmoil, she couldn't help but smile when Chris stuck his head around the edge of the door, looking handsome and normal in jeans and a T-shirt that was so nerdy that she had to roll her eyes.

Only Chris could pull off a T-shirt that had three different kinds of video game controllers on it with the caption *Choose Your Weapon*. Of course, it might have partially been because she had never seen someone with a T-shirt like that who also looked like he could have at least held his own in a real-life version of the games.

"Well, now, if it isn't Carl's favorite playmate," Tim teased, grinning. "What's up, Chris?"

"Tim," Chris greeted him back. "How is Carl, anyway?"

"Eating solid food now," Tim joked. "You?"

"Here on business." Chris turned his attention to Cassidy. "Um, hi, Cassidy."

"Uh-oh, business, really? I guess I better stay then," Tim joked, making Cassidy blush. She never, ever should have told her brothers even a single detail about her times with Chris. "Remember, Cassie, he's here for *business.*"

"Shut up, Tim." Cassidy felt heat flush her face. "So what's up, Chris?"

"I've got a bit of a business emergency." Chris leaned against the windowsill. "Andrew wants to put out an update to *Sky Adventures* in near-record time."

"So you're going to be too busy to see me for a while?" Cassidy asked, disappointed. "I mean, I get it, but—"

"Not that, and we'll figure something out," Chris said with so much certainty that Cassidy totally believed him. "I don't care if I have to see you doing nothing more than sitting out on the front porch. But it involves the B&B because we're bringing in a team. Now let me ask you, how many people can this place handle?"

"How are they sleeping?" Tim asked, and Chris tilted his head. "We've got ten rooms. Five of the rooms have beds we can separate into two twins, but another five have solid beds. Unless you're bringing in couples, they're solo sorts of rooms."

Chris went silent, combining what Tim had just told him with the facts in his head, nodding for a moment. "A question …

would it be a problem if two of the couples are ... nontraditional?"

"You mean unmarried or LGBT?" Cassidy asked, and Chris nodded. "Not a problem with me. We're country here in Saint Cloud, but most folks aren't that backward. Why?"

"Well, here's how it'd be," Chris said. "We want to rent the entire B&B for a solid month, starting next week. Every room, with breakfast service. I know that might mean some more cooking, but most of these folks are coders. You don't need gourmet to fill their bellies—half of them live off Hot Pockets and microwave pizza all the time anyway."

Cassidy gaped. Thirty days, even with a discounted room rate...

But something hit her. Why would Chris come here? There were other hotels in town; Saint Cloud was small but not *that* small. After all, if he was bringing in a dozen or more people, there were at least three other places she could think of that would be easier, maybe with conference room facilities and—

"Sounds good to me." Tim stood up before Cassidy could refuse Chris's offer. "The res book is pretty empty, and I'll get online and make sure all the sites know we're booked through."

"Wait a second." Cassidy bit her lip. She didn't want to argue with her brother in front of someone outside the family, even if Chris was her ... boyfriend. But that didn't mean she would just roll over and let Tim steamroll her. "Chris, I appreciate the offer, but business-wise, I need to look over the paperwork. I'm sure your company will be fair, but you understand this is a huge request for a B&B our size."

"No, I totally get it." Chris smiled easily. "Tell you what, Cass. How about I get the paperwork together, bring it by tomorrow afternoon? And then maybe you and I can have dinner together?"

"Sounds businesslike," Tim joked, but Chris shrugged. "Cassie?"

"Okay, okay. I'll be free after four o'clock, and Carl can man the phone if we get any calls. Does that make everyone happy?" Cassidy said, perhaps a bit more sharply than she intended. "Excuse me. That was rude."

Thankfully, Chris took it well and gave her a little smile. "Relax. I know I dropped a bomb into things, but I hope it's a good one. Either way, I'm looking forward to dinner tomorrow. How's that restaurant down the street sound, the Silver Lining?"

"Perfect." Cassidy smiled in relief. She got out of her chair, and when Chris bent down to give her a kiss on the cheek, she kissed his cheek back. "Tomorrow, cowboy."

Chris chuckled and left, and after she heard the door close, she turned on Tim, who'd stayed in his chair. "Don't you *ever* make an agreement on something like that without us talking it through first, you understand me?"

"Excuse me, Cassidy, but you sound like you're feeling a bit too big for your britches," Tim replied, his jaw set. "You're my big sister, and I love you and respect you. But you told me yourself this business is failing. Well, the numbers in my head are telling me that a fully booked month of rooms is more than we're going to make for the entire summer season."

"And?" Cassidy asked. "It's clearly a handout from Chris, who has guessed the situation we're in even if he doesn't know the actual figures. His family's the big new money in town, and he wants to make a good impression."

"So friggin' what?" Tim asked, angrier than Cassidy had seen him in a long time. Mama detested cursing, and while she knew her brother wasn't a choir boy with his mouth, he'd almost never curse around the house. This was the closest she'd seen him get in a long time. "Cassidy, who cares if the Davises want to splash their money in town? Sounds to me like Chris is going to bring those people in whether they stay here or not. So why not let him splash that money on us? At least that way it'd stay in town instead of going to some corporate office in Austin or out of state!"

"And what if we can't do it?" Cassidy asked. "A solid *month* of full bookings? My god, Tim, do you know how much work that'll be?"

"Do we look like the kind of people who don't like hard work?" Tim countered. He took a deep breath and stood up to take Cassidy's hands. "Cassie, look. You're right, I should have talked it over with you first. But we need this. And I know you—you won't let this be some sort of handout from the Davises. If anything, this might just be what this old place needs, give us the budget to breathe and implement some of the new ideas that we've had in mind."

Cassidy thought about it. She, Tim, and Carl had spitballed all sorts of ideas to renovate the building, to add in a coffee bar, other ways to bring in more business. None of them had gotten past the paper stage simply because of a lack of funds. "Maybe," she said reluctantly, and Tim grinned. "I said *maybe,* Tim. If the coders are going to be here a whole month, we might be able to try out some of the ideas. But I'm *not* letting you turn the dining room into a karaoke bar. You know those computer geeks are going to know nothing but 'Friends In Low Places' or 'Save a Horse, Ride a Cowboy.'"

"Speaking of cowboys," Tim said, grinning, "you gave Chris a nickname. Y'all are that serious, huh?"

"Nunya," Cassidy said, short for None of Your Business. Normally it worked.

Normally.

"Cassidy and Chris … C&C … ooh, I know!" Tim said, suddenly making weird noises. It took Cassidy a few moments, but she eventually recognized the tune, a moldy oldie she hadn't heard since high school. "Gonna Make You Sweat," by C&C Music Factory.

"Not even!" she growled, and Tim stopped, laughing.

"Okay, okay. Tell you what. You run some numbers. Carl and I will do the same on some ideas for trials we can run while the coders are here. Then we can discuss it tomorrow before Chris gets here with the contracts. How's that sound?"

Cassidy nodded, knowing it was the best she could get out of her brother at the moment. "Yeah. Hey, you keeping Carl honest on his ankle?"

Tim snorted. "What do you think that man's doing right now? Seems getting dumped in the lake lit a fire under him I ain't seen since football."

Cassidy thought about it and nodded in approval. "Good."

CHAPTER 13

"This is nice," Chris said as they entered the Silver Lining restaurant. He was impressed. A medium-sized, intimate restaurant, the Silver Lining was a neo-indigenous or Spanish building with lots of arched passageways done in stucco or adobe style, he wasn't sure which. The bits of exposed roof beams looked real too, not faux round "ancient wood" style, but thick four-by-sixes that were squared off and stained dark to contrast with the pale salmon of the walls.

"Yeah, the Silvers have a really good sense of style." Cassidy looped her arm through his. "They were one of the first families to look at reinvigorating Dusty Bend and decided to build instead of renovate. Oh, you should have been around for the arguments that people got into about *that!*"

"Like what?" Chris asked curiously, wondering if his own family was going to be walking into a similar situation.

"Oh, the arguments went on and on in the local paper, even at city council meetings," Cassidy said. "I can't remember them all really; so many of them were ridiculous. Like I remember one woman saying that by using the traditional construction techniques the Silvers wanted to use, the building would be unsafe, that it would dissolve in the first big rainstorm that hit."

Chris laughed. "Um, and just how did people live before steel-framed aluminum-sided buildings then?"

"I don't know, considering my place is all wood construction," Cassidy pointed out. "In the end, it was like a lot of arguments here in town, the new versus the old."

"And I'm very new," Chris pointed out as they sat down at a table. The Silver Lining wasn't exactly a restaurant, not exactly a sports bar either. If he had to classify it, he'd call it a casual evening place. "My whole company is."

"Trust me," Cassidy said with a chuckle, "when the traditionalists start seeing the investment you and yours are making into Saint Cloud, they'll come around. They fought the wineries, saying they were taking away from the traditional small farms that used to be there until folks saw the jobs and the tourism money the wineries produced. People fought the Silvers until they saw that this place was pretty good and that Dusty Bend was rejuvenating. They'll probably fight you too until they see the jobs that you'll bring to town."

"Change is hard," Chris said, and Cassidy nodded. "Speaking of changes, thanks for not rejecting the room offer. I could tell last night you weren't on board at first."

"It's okay," Cassidy said. "Truth is, Chris, I'm trying to figure out how to change myself. I know that I can't just keep doing things the way I am. The B&B won't support it; my family can't survive that way. In fact, before you came in, Tim and I were talking about him leaving to go find another job."

"Not because he's suddenly filled with an intense desire to become an insurance salesman, I'm sure," Chris said, and Cassidy shook her head. "So change happens either way. What changed your mind?"

"That if change was going to happen, I wanted to be in charge of it, have some form of control," Cassidy said before smiling. "And to be honest, your brother didn't try to negotiate the room rates down too much. We had a bigger discount through the website."

"I won't tell Andrew if you won't." Chris laughed. A waitress came over, and they placed their order, and as they waited, Chris noticed a band setting up on stage. "Live music?"

"One of the changes to Dusty Bend that the Silvers started and now pretty much everyone copies," Cassidy said. "Every coffee shop, restaurant, event space, or what has some sort of live music. Actually, you chose a good spot; the Silvers hire good bands. I don't know which one has the ear for talent, but they've got it."

The band started up, and Chris had to agree with Cassidy. They were good. "I wouldn't say they're Santana, but there's not really anyone like Carlos Santana."

Cassidy nodded. "Very true. Besides, Santana's a bit too loud for this place. You just can't play the electric guitar like that properly without turning it up."

"Good point."

The music was more than good, Chris decided. It was rock, with a blues and Latin twist to it that didn't quite land the band in any one category but stayed with him even as he and Cassidy sipped their drinks. After setting his glass down, he reached across the table, taking her hand and rubbing a thumb across the back of her fingers. "Thank you."

"For what?"

Chris smiled, feeling a warmth in his chest that had nothing to do with the temperature or the music. "For giving a total stranger from out of town a chance. It's still hard to believe at times."

"I should be the one thanking you," Cassidy replied. "You could have had any girl in Saint Cloud. Yet you showed up to sand my rockers."

"Some people hearing that could think it's some sort of euphemism," Chris joked, and Cassidy blushed. "I'm just saying."

"Well, let's just say that it's been on my mind, yes," Cassidy said. "What are your views on … sanding?"

Chris took a deep breath and thought for a moment before replying. Despite the light tone, he knew this was a serious subject that they both needed to address. And, to be honest, have fun with too. There was nothing wrong with what they were thinking about; it just had to be approached respectfully. "I told you before, in college things were easy. Too easy. And I won't lie to you—I've sanded a few chairs in my time. My sander's thankfully clean, though, and I want to keep it that way. So I've come to a decision that if and when the time is right, it's going to be good and with the right chair. You?"

Cassidy took a breath and gave his hand a squeeze. "I've been sanded once before. I don't regret it, but I'm like you. I want sanding to mean something. And I'm not going to ask about your technique."

Chris grinned. "Actually, you could," he said playfully before leaning in to whisper in her ear. "Miss Norton, when I sand, I sand right."

"Well, it's been a long time since my last sanding." Cassidy's voice caught slightly.

"Mine too," Chris admitted. "But I'm in no rush, Cassidy. When we decide the time is right, it'll be right for both of us. And mean something."

Cassidy's eyes gleamed, and she gave his hand another squeeze. "You know, it's hard for me to accept help. I was always the big sister, and after Mama passed and Daddy had his stroke, I had to be the strong one. You showing up the way you did, and now the rentals … I'm not saying I'm ungrateful. I am saying that I might chafe sometimes out of fear."

"I'm afraid too," Chris admitted. "But like you said, I'm more afraid of what would happen if I didn't try. I'll admit I don't get it all. I'm not the oldest—I had a few good years where I was the baby of the family. Then when I saw Dylan for the first time? I liked being a big brother. I was sort of in that happy spot where I could be the big brother, but Andrew was the one who really was the real big brother, you know?"

Cassidy nodded. "You got the best of both worlds. No middle child syndrome?"

"Nah," Chris said with a laugh. "That's Brian's role. But really, my brothers and I have gotten along pretty well. We're each close enough in age that hanging out together was never that awkward, but far enough apart that we weren't stepping on each other's toes, trying to date the same girls in school. I mean, by the time I was old enough to figure out just how wonderful and amazing girls were, Andrew was already in college."

"And did he ever have a cute girlfriend you crushed on?" Cassidy asked, and Chris shrugged, saying nothing. She smiled. "Thought so."

"Now the shoe's on the other foot," Chris pointed out. "He can be jealous that I've got the gorgeous, vivacious girlfriend while he's got … well, right now he's got a bunch of spreadsheets."

"You think that'll last a long time?" Cassidy asked. "I'd be surprised."

Chris considered and chuckled as he thought about the similarities between him and Andrew. "I think Andrew's a lot like me, as much as we might seem different at times. He had his playful time, but he's moved on. I'm not saying he's going to settle down with the first girl that catches his fancy, but at the same time I wouldn't be surprised if he did. If she's the right person."

"And you?" Cassidy asked. "What do you see in your future?"

Chris pursed his lips. "A lot." He stopped to think for a few seconds. "With the right woman, I would love to have kids, build a home, a family. The Cloud 9 is a huge property. I could see taking an acre for myself and my family, building a house. Heck, if they want, I'll even teach the kids to ride."

Cassidy snorted. "Not with the way you ride."

"I caught you, didn't I?"

The music changed from a happy bluesy vibe to something slower, more intimate and romantic, and Cassidy squeezed his hand. "Maybe I'll let you catch me next time. So, Mr. Horse-Riding-Chair-Sander, can you dance?"

"Dance?" Chris asked, and Cassidy nodded, standing up. "I've been known to cut a rug or two in my day."

Chris stood up and led Cassidy to what was clearly the dance floor of the place. It wasn't big, just enough for three or four couples, but he didn't care. As he took her in his arms and her hands rested on his shoulders, he felt a warmth ignite. It wasn't just the fire of desire and passion, although as they moved to the intimate Latin-infused music, he could feel his body reacting to the closeness of the beautiful woman in his arms.

It was the look in her eyes, the way he could see forever reflected in the twin beautiful orbs. It was in the way her fingers caressed the back of his neck in that spot between the collar of his shirt and his hairline.

It was the way she stepped closer, her softness pressing against his body as he pulled her near. Every curve was luscious; every soft inhalation of her scent left his head spinning and his heart pounding in his chest.

He ran a hand up her spine, feeling the slight texture of her frame through the cotton of her shirt and the softness of her skin, and Cassidy bit her lip, her eyes darkening with want as he caressed her.

When the song was over, he leaned in, not caring if they were in public. Let all of Saint Cloud see; they probably were already whispering. He was going to kiss his girlfriend, and as Cassidy kissed him back, he could feel something wash over him that was more than just desire or heat.

It was total belonging.

He barely tasted any of dinner, not really caring about it. Instead they talked—about the future, about town, about the next few weeks as they prepared for the intense hustle of getting the online update for *Sky* out.

Instead of driving back to the bed and breakfast, they walked the few blocks, hand in hand, until they reached the porch, where Chris pulled her close again. "Thank you for a wonderful evening."

Cassidy put her arms around his neck, pushing him back slightly until his back was pressed against one of the railing posts and their bodies molded against each other. "You can definitely dance with me anytime you want," she said before kissing him once more. He opened up to her, his hands drifting below her belt line to cup the denim-clad curve of her hip.

When she pulled back, they were both breathing heavily, their eyes dark with want. "Chris," Cassidy whispered.

"Let's listen to the parts of us who want to wait," Chris replied, and she nodded. "I feel the same way. Cass, I have never in my entire life wanted a woman more than I want you right now, right here. But I want to wait, not because I don't want you, not because I don't think making love with you would be the most intense experience of my life. But because I want more. I'm greedy for you, Cassidy Norton."

"Greedy?" Cassidy whispered, and Chris nodded.

"When we go there, when we fully join as man and woman," he whispered into her ear, brushing her hair back and inhaling her scent, "I promise you, Cassidy Norton, that we're going to go there because it's going to mean something permanent.

We'll both be forever changed by what happens, and because the world will be different for us afterwards."

Cassidy nodded. He wouldn't go inside with her, but as his lips traced the soft skin of her neck and to her jawline, he could imagine the change.

"Chris, I want that too," Cassidy moaned, her fingers hooking to scratch at the back of his neck. "But I think kissing is okay, right?"

Chris chuckled and kissed her throat again, feeling the throb of her pulse under his lips. "I think we can sneak kisses as much as we want out here. Or at the ranch."

Cassidy hummed and lowered her chin to kiss him on the lips again. For long, intense minutes, their bodies pressed against each other, their lips saying things that didn't need words, their tongues forming poetry that was beyond human speech. Instead, they communicated on a level beyond the shackles of language, their hands exploring and tracing each other through their clothes.

Chris could feel his heart swell. Here was someone he could see in his arms forever, and when the porch light flipped on and off a few times, causing them to step apart, they were both breathless ... and giggling.

"I think we were being watched in the living room," Chris whispered, looking toward the darkened window. Cassidy shook her head. "No?"

"No ... security camera over the door," she said, cutting her eyes up and over her shoulder. "The display's right there next to the check-in computer."

"I see. Well, let them watch," Chris said. "But I understand. Don't want to give this place a reputation or anything."

Cassidy giggled. "Nope, I'd rather give the Cloud 9 ranch a reputation anyway. Better for my business."

Chris leaned his head back, laughing. "Point taken. More privacy too. No security cameras. Well, until then. Goodnight, Cassidy."

"Goodnight, Chris," Cassidy said, backing up. She didn't turn around, fumbling with the screen door behind her back until she could find the latch. With a final blown kiss, she stepped inside, Chris staying on the porch until the light went out.

Only then did he carefully make his way down the steps. He was going to need to jump in the lake before going inside, that was for sure.

CHAPTER 14

"Excuse me, miss?" the man asked Cassidy as she scrubbed down the dining-room table, trying to get out a ring of what she thought might have been oatmeal. She wasn't quite sure; it was a lot stickier than any oatmeal residue she'd ever dealt with before.

"Yes, how can I help you?" she asked, looking up at the man. He was one of the *code monkeys*, a status he wore loud and proud on his T-shirt, which had a picture of a chimpanzee banging on a keyboard above a caption that read *PEBKAC: Problem Exists Between Keyboard And Chair.*

It seemed disrespectful and patronizing all at once, but it wasn't even the weirdest thing she'd seen over the past two days. The new guest who wore fishnet stockings under her shorts while relaxing in the rockers on the porch was probably the weirdest.

"Does your laundry service use hypoallergenic all-natural detergent?" he asked nervously. "I've got to have my lucky T-shirt ready to go tomorrow, or else I won't be able to match my aura to the room!"

Cassidy blinked, not quite understanding. "Your … aura?"

"Yeah!" the man said happily. "Someone gets it! So, like, do you have it?"

"Um … we use the supermarket brand," she admitted. "I don't think stores around Saint Cloud sell all-natural detergent."

The man's face fell, and Cassidy felt bad for him. Thinking quickly, she raised a finger. "But I've got an idea," she said. "The store does sell baking soda, and my mama always taught me that nothing gets out stains like a baking soda soak!"

"Bicarbonate of soda," the man mused, apparently comparing the idea to his personal list of issues. "Yeah, yeah, that'll work!"

"Okay," Cassidy said, relieved. "You bring your laundry down to the front desk before you go to work today, and I'll swing by the store to get a big box of baking soda. You'll have your shirt by the time you get back tonight."

One brushfire put out, Cassidy moved on to the next: breakfast. Despite Chris's assurances that his team would be satisfied with simple, basic breakfasts, the idea of serving nothing but instant oatmeal and microwave-cup breakfasts made her shiver on the inside.

But the *requests* from the team left her wondering just how well these new people would fit in town. Saint Cloud was the sort of live-and-let-live town where most people ate bacon and eggs for breakfast, and if you didn't, your neighbors wouldn't bother you and you wouldn't bother your neighbors.

The code team was … not that. There was one coder, a slightly built woman who had pink hair that was shaved on one side of her head, who, from what Cassidy could tell, didn't eat anything. Or maybe her diet consisted of the pot of bean sprouts she'd found in the room when she'd come through with the vacuum cleaner the day before.

There were times that Cassidy wondered if she knew what she'd gotten herself into. On the other hand, the account book hadn't seen so much good news in a very long time. It was hypnotic, looking at that huge deposit in the bank account, knowing what it meant.

Even the name on the account meant something to her. Not Big Sky Games, but Cloud 9 Studios. It told Cassidy that the Davis brothers were looking long term, that they were invested in Saint Cloud.

That Chris was invested in her.

So it made the challenges worth it. Besides, other than the occasional extra trip to the supermarket for extra cleaning supplies, certain other jobs were easier. The rooms only had to be cleaned once every three days, and linens were changed once a week.

It balanced out.

"Hey, Cass?"

She turned, seeing Carl come down the hallway. Of the three Nortons, Carl had had the hardest time dealing with the coding team. Apparently, someone had heard about Carl's ankle injury, and he'd twice been offered help, once with a chakra cleanse, another with yoga.

It was all well-meaning, but Cassidy knew her brother was walking on eggshells. "What's up, Carl?"

"Look." He leaned against the wall and jammed his hands in his pockets, "You mind if I get out of here for the day? I mean, these folks are okay, but… I mean, one of them was giving me stink eye for eating a steak for breakfast."

"Steak for breakfast?" Cassidy asked, and Carl shrugged. "Really?"

"Hey, it's been a long time since we've had anything but hamburger or rabbit sausage," Carl pointed out. "And it was a small one. Anyway, I've got to get around some regular people again."

Cassidy thought, and an idea came to mind. "What about going out to the Cloud 9?" she asked. "I bet you go out there, talk to the foreman or Andrew Davis, and they'll put you to work. Get an honest day's sweat in, might even have some more steak money in your pocket at the end of the day."

Carl chuckled. "You really are starting to trust these Davis boys, aren't you?"

"They're doing okay so far, even if they're new in town," Cassidy said honestly. "Nobody's said anything about them yet, even if they're not fully Saint Cloud people at this time. And I trust Chris."

Carl's smile faded, and he gave Cassidy a serious, introspective look. "You've got feelings for him, don't you? Real feelings?"

Cassidy smiled and zipped her lips. "You're being a nosy little brother."

She knew she was avoiding the topic, but that was because she just wasn't sure how to label how she felt about Chris. She'd grown up in Saint Cloud, and her years of college weren't enough to shake some of those homespun ideas from her soul. In her mind, she and Chris were walking the right path, the way a couple was supposed to be.

But she wasn't sure she could trust the intensity of how she felt about him. He left her feeling like a high school girl on her first crush, ready to draw little hearts everywhere and maybe carve proof of their dating on a tree somewhere.

She wasn't a girl in high school, though. She was a fully grown woman, and that made her wary. Still, she knew Chris was good and that she felt good when she was with him.

And somehow, her little brother understood. "I'm happy for you, Cassie."

"What do you mean, Carl?" she asked, and Carl chuckled.

"You know, the world ain't fair," Carl said, and Cassidy nodded. "Everyone's got their patch of fire to walk through. Some of us, it's a short patch, barely a suntan. Some of us, it's a patch that seems to last their whole life. You've been dealing with your patch for almost a decade, and I'm not happy to say I've been some of that fire."

"Carl, you needed help. You're a good man."

"Who ain't done with sweeping up after my fire's burned out," Carl said simply. "But that's okay, this is about you. Now this Chris Davis, he's treated you right. He makes you happy. So it's good. You deserve happiness."

"Yeah, but … it's hard to see a future in both this place and with him. I mean Carl, what if he wants to do some of that billionaire business life? Trips to Tahiti, skiing in Sweden or something?"

"Then pack sunscreen and enjoy it," Carl said simply, laughing softly. "Cassie, this place, it's just a building. Yeah, our parents bought this place. They kept it running. But this place was lots of things before we Nortons owned it. And who knows if it'll be something different in the future? I don't, and you don't. So if life, and happiness, takes you on a different path, I'll be there to cheer you on."

Cassidy's throat tightened, and she looked at her brother with tears brimming in her eyes. "Carl … but what about you? You said you're still sweeping up."

"I am, and I'll probably keep doing so. You never know. I might even have a couple of times I might give you a holler for a helping hand. I've learned not to be so stubborn that I can't get a little help when needed."

"You do have a hard head."

Carl laughed softly. "Runs in the family. Cassie, I know what folks in town think of me. And I ain't gonna lie, some of that is deserved. I was in a dark, dark place when I came back from college. But I can't sit under your umbrella forever, letting my big sister shelter me from all of the rainstorms that'll come my way. Your path takes you away from this place, you go. Don't worry about me. Don't doubt yourself for a second. I'll make things happen. I'll be fine. Maybe what I need is to grow up a little more on my own now anyways."

Cassidy reached out, hugging her brother. Even though he towered over her, she'd always think of him as her little brother, the boy whose knee she'd clean after he'd scraped it out in the yard.

But he was more than that, and she had to recognize that fact. He was a man now, and she loved him just as he was. "You know I'll always be here for you, Carl."

"I know, Cassie," he said, kissing the top of her head. "But right now, I'm going to go get my head clear, okay?"

"Okay." She stepped back and wiped her eyes. "Say, as long as you're heading out, you mind dropping me off at the market? I need to pick up a few things, and I can walk back."

"You sure?" Carl asked dubiously. "It's mighty warm out."

"Now, Carl Norton, you can't go and make that growing up on your own speech and then worry about me having to walk a mile in the sunshine," Cassidy said with a small laugh. "I'll be fine. I just need to pick up some baking soda and borax."

"What for?"

Cassidy chuckled. "I'll tell you in the truck."

CHAPTER 15

Walking through the large open room his brother had rented—a former agricultural warehouse if what he'd heard was correct—Chris could see his team was fading.

Some of that was to be expected. They'd all been putting in ten-hour days minimum for a full week, nobody more so than Chris. He'd gotten used to rolling out of bed at five in the morning, doing a quick exercise session to get his body and mind going, and rolling into the office by seven, eating a ham and cheese biscuit as he drove.

From there, it was pedal to the metal until at least seven PM, but he didn't mind. In his ethos, leaders led from the front, and that meant if he was going to ask his workers to put in long hours, he needed to be ready to do the same thing.

The hardest part for him had been only being able to swap text messages with Cassidy most days. The rented space was less than a half mile from the bed and breakfast, making it torturous for him. He wanted to be down the street, spending time with Cassidy and learning everything he could about her.

And instead, the most he'd been able to do in the past week was two lunches eaten on the porch of the house. Unsatisfying, to say the least.

But on that Saturday afternoon, his problem wasn't his lack of time with Cassidy. It was his team. They were tapering off, and while he understood their tiredness, they were only six days into the project.

There was a lot of work still to be done.

"Okay, hands off the keyboards," he called out loudly, striding toward the middle of the room. "Come on in, group meeting."

He could see the wariness in his team's eyes, but they'd been working together for a long time. He'd recruited the best of the best, and he'd earned their trust in their time together. So it was with careful trust that they gathered around the big conference table that dominated the center of the space, some of the team pausing to refill their bottles with one of the drink options on hand. They were averaging five gallons of G Fuel a day, and Chris had fresh shipments coming into the ranch daily.

But G Fuel and good chairs weren't enough, and he could see it in his crew's eyes. So he started with a nod, knowing they deserved some kudos.

"First off, everyone, I want to say thank you. You've all come here to Saint Cloud on short notice, and have been working your butts off. Don't think I don't see that. You're an All-Star team because I knew you could do it. But let's be honest … y'all need a reset."

"Yeah," Jenae said, her pink hair hanging a lot more limply than normal, "turn us off and turn our butts back on again."

There were a few chuckles, but more groans of understanding than Chris would have liked. He looked across the table at Simon, who nodded. He knew what everyone was feeling, but Simon had an advantage. He was at least partly at home here. The rest of the team wasn't, and they needed to vent.

"Okay, well, as much as I'd like to stock defibrillators in the break room, I don't think OSHA would approve." Chris sat down. "So how about we do something that may be a little more difficult, but also in the long term more helpful. Gripe session."

"Gripe session?" Payton, with a pale face and volcanic expression, asked, brightening. "Where do we start?"

"Well, first, some ground rules," Chris said. "Rule one, anything said right now stays here. Actions are to be taken by me and my brothers unless we say so. Rule two, interpersonal beef is to be handled between you and the team member you're beefing with. If you need a third party, you talk to Simon or myself. But we're not going to start looking like a *Real Housewives* reunion around here. Third, while we all acknowledge and accept our feelings, try to keep your words to being as neutral as possible. Other than that, take turns and let's hear it out. The floor is yours. This is a safe space for all of you."

Chris knew he was taking a risk, but if his team trusted him, he trusted them just as much. He trusted that they'd focus on the matter at hand and stay as professional as they could.

The first person to speak up was Takeshi, who'd been with the company the longest and had been one of the original animation coders for *Sky Adventures*. "I think the biggest issue I've had is that I feel like I'm not fitting in."

"You've got that right," Pete, another coder, said. "Feel like I'm under a microscope every time I walk out of this room."

There were nods all around the table, and Chris felt a very real tremor of concern inside. His team was diverse, culturally different from small-town Saint Cloud. While they'd accepted him and his brothers, maybe asking them to come out here was too much.

"Has anyone said anything … prejudiced to you guys?" Chris asked worriedly. "If so, that's something I need to know so we can get it addressed. You know my policy on bullying."

The team nodded again; in fact, Chris was famous for it. Despite, or maybe because of, the general background of coders as being geeks and misfits, cruelty and bullying were often rampant in the tech industry. Chris had heard the horror stories when he'd been in college, and when it was time to make *Sky* market ready, he'd sworn that he wasn't going to let it happen to him.

So respect was the name of his game. And while tolerance was sometimes uncomfortable and often a challenge for him, the more he practiced it, the better he got at it. In fact, the only things he didn't tolerate amongst his teams were lack of performance, lack of effort, and lack of respect for themselves or others.

"Chris, I don't think it's anything you can put into words, at least not in my case," Laura, one of the other female coders on the team, said. "But it's like this general cold shoulder that we get. Like the other night after we left, I walked down to the Mexican restaurant that's just past the boarding house we're staying in. And when I asked if their tortillas are made with heritage corn or not, they just sort of looked at me like they didn't understand what I was saying."

Across the table, Chris could see Simon snicker, and when Laura looked at him, he held up a hand. "Sorry, Laura, it's just that … well, this is Saint Cloud. A lot of folks around here may not know what heritage corn is, and they for sure don't know where to source that from even if they do know what heritage corn is."

"But … are you saying that they're using *GMO food*?" Laura asked in soft horror. "Don't they know what that'll do to their pineal gland?"

"Laura, a lot of folks around here aren't thinking like that," Simon said honestly. "They won't stop you from trying to get your pineal gland healthy, but for a lot of them, they're worried about putting enough food in their stomach to get through the day, regardless of how much genetics are involved."

Laura opened her mouth to argue but sighed, nodding. "I'm going to be ordering a lot of stuff online, won't I?"

"We'll work with you," Chris assured her. "All of you. In fact, I'm giving you all homework. Tomorrow is a day off. You don't have to be in here. But by noon tomorrow, I want you all to text me at least one thing you want that you haven't been able to find here in town. Let's see what we can do about either getting it brought in or, better yet, locally sourced. You'd be surprised at what a town like this might have tucked away in some side street."

"Still, I feel like a square peg," Hamish, a big burly Scotsman on the team, said. "I can take the sun, I can take the horrible beer. But they don't understand me when I say something!"

"Hamish, you're from Glasgow," Takeshi said with a smile. "It took me two months to learn to understand you. These Texans? You're about as intelligible as when I speak Japanese."

That earned a laugh all around, and Chris joined in. "Okay, I think I'm sensing a general trend. You're not feeling accepted. Now, quick question, has anyone said anything to you specifically?"

Seeing shaking heads around the table, he let out a sigh of relief. "Thank goodness on that one. But seriously, everyone, if *anyone* says something that makes you feel uncomfortable or whatever, I want to know about it. Agreed?"

There were nods around the table, but at the end, Carson, another team member, raised his hand. "What about looks? I mean, nobody's saying anything, but it's the *looks*, Chris. Like we don't belong here."

Chris nodded, even though, in his eyes, he could see why Carson was getting looks. The man was wearing sweatpants with spangly red suspenders. "I'll see what I can do, Carson. But may I suggest around the table that while there's a lot to be said for taking a stand, a little camouflage doesn't hurt, either. You see me in jeans and a T-shirt, right? Y'all can do the same."

"How … boring." Jenae shrugged. "Whatever. You didn't say what kind of T-shirt."

"That's the spirit. Take a step toward the mountain, and the mountain'll take ten steps toward you," he misquoted, knowing he was mangling it but not really worried about it. "Now get the heck out of here. Save where you are, shut it down, and I'll see you all on Monday."

That earned at least a little cheer from the team, and in a few minutes the room was cleared except for Chris and Simon, who sat easily in his work chair, leaning back with his "coding Nikes" propped up on the desk in front of him. "So what do you think?"

"I think that we've got a bit of a pickle," Chris admitted. "The team is the best around, but you know how code geeks are."

"Geeks," Simon said with a grin, and Chris nodded. "Saint Cloud ain't a town for geeks."

"I wonder, though," Chris said. "It's not accepting ten geeks. But you know the team, Simon. They're good people. A little unique at times, but good people. What about when we bring in another thousand geeks?"

"At that point you're going to have a bigger issue on your hands," Simon said honestly. "Chris, this town ... Look, the people here are good people. But they're stubborn, especially if they think they're getting pressured from outside. Doesn't matter how much money we bring in, what you want to donate to the school district, or jobs we hand out. If the town thinks they're getting forced into something they don't want, they'll dig their heels in."

"Now you tell me?" Chris asked, and Simon shrugged. Chris sighed, knowing that Simon was right. He'd already anticipated it; he just didn't think it could happen this quickly. "So we need to bring folks together. Ideas?"

"What about ... what about a touch football game?" Simon said. "This town, it's football crazy. We're in Texas, after all."

Chris hummed. "And I remember the last company picnic, a game got going. Folks had a lot of fun, too."

"It's a bridge that both sides can cross," Simon said before laughing. "Imagine what some of these local folks will think when Carson goes flying for a touchdown with those suspenders of his sparkling in the sun."

Chris laughed, knowing what Simon meant. Carson might have dressed eccentrically, but he was a former college track and field runner who specialized in the four-hundred-meter hurdles. Even if he was a step or two slower than in his college days, he still could outsprint most people without a problem.

"One thing, though," Chris said. "Now, between the team and the two of us, that's twelve. My brothers thrown in, and maybe Matt Miller, that's seventeen. But we need folks from town."

"You could get the Nortons."

"Two locals and seventeen of us ... No, we'll need more." Chris tapped the table. "Who else can we call in?"

"You want my opinion, call up City Hall. Amelia Hernandez will owe you a favor because of the rent you've dropped into Dusty Bend. Kim Johnson'll want you on her side come next election. And I suspect if you ask the local police and fire department, they'll be up for it."

"A good idea. I'll chat up Andrew on that," Chris said. "In the meantime, you get the heck out of here too. You've earned it."

"So says the guy working twelve-plus hours a day," Simon said. "Piece of advice, Chris. Cassidy's a hard-working woman; she understands you're busy. But take an extra few minutes a day to have lunch with her frequently. She'll appreciate that."

Chris chuckled. "What do you think tomorrow is? Don't call me unless something's burning."

Simon and Chris split up, Simon taking the evening for himself while Chris drove back to the ranch. He found his brothers in the main house, all of them sweaty. Especially Dylan, who was still getting used to town.

"You look like a man who's gotten his solid day in," Chris said as he came in, grabbing a big glass and going to the fridge to pour himself some milk. "What'd you do?"

"Work on the stables with Carl Norton," Dylan said, getting his own glass of tea. "Man's a machine. Which we need; Justin Logan's bringing a horse on Monday."

"Andrew struck a deal with him too, huh?" Chris asked, and Dylan nodded. "Cool. So where is Andrew, anyway?"

"Home office," Dylan said. "How's the programming going?"

"It's been a good week, but that's what I need to talk to Andrew about," Chris said, heading deeper into the house. More work had gotten done, and when he got to Andrew's home office, he had to admit that his brother looked right at home in his big chair, headphones on as he watched a movie on his big computer screen. "Hey, Andrew."

"'Sup, Chris?" Andrew asked as he paused the movie and popped out his headphones. "Good Saturday?"

"Yes and no," Chris said. "Team's tired and feeling like they're not fitting in. But they've done a lot of good work over the past six days."

Andrew sat up, breathing through his nose. "Not fitting in?"

"Face it, Andrew, they're not country boys like us," Chris said. "Or at least, we were suburbanish. Hamish is from the lowlands of Scotland, Takeshi's from San Francisco, Jenae is … well, Jenae."

It was meant as a joke, but Andrew didn't laugh. If anything, his forehead grew more cloudy. "You wouldn't have come to me this easily if you didn't have an idea."

"I do," Chris said. "Touch football."

Andrew sat back, surprised. "Explain."

Chris did, going over the entire conversation before going over his ideas for the football game. Andrew nodded along, asking questions from time to time, but at the end he was smiling. "And you think this'll get the town to accept the coders?"

"I think it'll be helpful," Chris said. "Look at it this way. The coders play well; they earn respect that way. They take a beating … well, if they do it without complaint, it'll earn respect too. And I'll talk with them, get them on board. I think it can work."

"Me too. But I'll put in a few more calls than what you suggest. Not just City Hall, but I'll call Justin Logan and Amanda Munoz. I bet they've got a few ranch hands that'll love a good game of football."

"And what about you?" Chris said. "You got the wind and speed to play a football game here in town?"

Andrew grinned and stood up. "So asks the guy who's not sleeping enough and spends twelve hours a day hunched over a computer. I bet Dylan could beat you right now, considering what he's been doing all week."

"Oh, is that a challenge?" Chris asked, and Andrew grinned. "Okay then, we'll just see. You're going to have a dozen highly motivated, dedicated computer geeks ready to go for a game. Combined, we're unstoppable."

"We'll see then, won't we?" Andrew challenged. "In the meantime, I've got a movie to finish watching."

Chris stood up, both amused and a little angry. Maybe he had been pushing his body for the update to the game.

But he had enough left in the tank to show Andrew that he could still hold his own on the football field too.

CHAPTER 16

It was early for their date; in fact, Chris was supposed to come pick Cassidy up. But after hearing the rumors and the talk of the folks at the bed and breakfast, she just couldn't contain herself any longer. Changing into some casual athletic shorts and a T-shirt that may have been a bit too youthful for her age, she borrowed an item from Tim's room before driving out to the Cloud 9 ranch, looking for answers.

Pulling around back, she saw a new face come out of the house, a tall, dirty-blond guy in a tank top and board shorts. She got out of the truck and approached as he gave a wave. "'Sup?"

"Hi, I'm Cassidy Norton," Cassidy introduced herself. "You're … not Dylan, I suppose?"

The tall guy laughed, stepping forward and offering a hand. He towered over Cassidy, a feeling she was unfamiliar with. He had to be at least six and a half feet tall, maybe even more with the way his chin cleared the top of her head easily. "Nope,

Dylan went into town to find something or the other. Matt Miller. And you're Chris's girlfriend."

"I am," she said, feeling warm inside at the comment. She was Chris's girlfriend, and it felt good to be part of a relationship again. More importantly, she felt good to be in a relationship with Chris. Since her conversation with Carl, she'd felt herself relaxing, enjoying the growth of their minds, hearts, and souls slowly exploring each other.

At least, that was the way she felt.

And the kissing was good too. She knew when the time came, lying with Chris as man and woman was going to be more than she'd ever thought possible.

But right now she had this big giant in front of her, looking very out of place in the dusty Texas sunshine. "So do you know where Chris is?" she asked, and Matt nodded.

"He took his new horse out for a morning ride," Matt said. "I figure he'll be back in a half hour, but I can give him a call if you want. Was he expecting you?"

"We were going to get together later today, but I heard about the football game idea and had to see if it was real."

Matt laughed. "Totally real. So who blabbed about it?"

"One of the coders staying at my place. She said she ran into Simon last night at dinner, and Simon filled her in on the idea. Nothing's set in stone yet."

"Not yet. Over breakfast Andrew said he was going to go make some calls, while Brian said he needed to get his butt in shape," Matt said. "Me? I figure they'll do what they did in college, just have me run downcourt and grab jump balls."

"Well, you do look like a basketball player," Cassidy noted. "Am I wrong?"

"In high school, but I played volleyball in college." Matt laughed. "Six-foot-eight is too short for being a center, and I don't have a decent jump shot past ten feet. That's okay, volleyball's more fun anyway."

"You might have a problem trying to find a game around here," Cassidy admitted. "I think the only volleyball teams around are the high school girls."

"No problem, I was thinking of volunteering to coach anyway," Matt said. "But for today, I'm going to drag my kayak out of the barn and go paddle around some. It's a small lake, but big enough to enjoy things. And … oh, I see Chris coming over the hill now."

Cassidy turned and did see Chris atop a new horse, a black one, and she felt a smile stretching her lips even before Chris caught sight of her and waved. Walking over to the stable, she met him just as he rode up, dismounting and pulling her in for a kiss.

"Oooh, you smell!" she playfully teased even as she ran her hands over his sweaty shirt, feeling his chest. While he did smell, it was a clean, honest, masculine smell. It was the smell of a man who'd been out doing something physical and real. It smelled like Chris, and it smelled good. "So is this your new baby?"

"You're my baby," Chris said simply, smiling. "And this is Noche, our newest horse. I wanted to take her out for a morning ride before Dylan takes everyone out for an afternoon in the paddock. I didn't expect to see you out here; weren't we going to meet up later? If I remember right, ice cream was the plan?"

"That *was* the plan until I heard you wanted to play football," Cassidy said. "Won't be any ice cream in your future. I know how my brothers will play."

"I thought Carl couldn't play anymore?" Chris asked. "His leg?"

"Not strong enough to play college ball, but he's as stubborn as an old mule. He'll tape it up and be out there for sure. And don't even think that touch rules will matter to him," Cassidy said. "Or anyone else around here."

"Point taken." Chris chuckled. "So ... after we get Noche here brushed down and relaxed, would you like to stick around and have lunch? Nothing fancy, but I could formally introduce you to all my brothers."

Cassidy stopped, joy and nervousness bursting inside her at the same time. While she'd met Brian and Andrew, and, of course, Simon, this was an invitation to a family meal. Did Chris realize that, as far as she was concerned, that meant a new level of seriousness to their relationship? "Really?"

He nodded and set down the stiff-bristled brush that he'd just picked up for Noche. "Really," he came over. "You're my lady, Cassidy. Plain and simple. You're on my mind every night when I go to sleep and on my mind every morning when I wake up. Every text message we can swap brightens my day, and every meal we can't share is like a punch to my gut. And my brothers know they'd better be on their best behavior."

"Then ... let's do it," Cassidy answered before she could lose her nerve. "And can I help with Noche?"

Chris got her another brush, and together they groomed the horse. She was a beautiful mare, docile and sweet, and Cassidy giggled when she reached out almost daintily with her lips to take a sugar cube from Cassidy's hand. Chris rubbed the mare's nose, smiling. "She likes you."

"Better be careful here, Mr. Davis. I might want Noche for myself."

"Okay."

Cassidy stopped, her eyes widening slightly. "Chris, I was joking."

"I wasn't." Chris took her hand. "You want Noche? Then she'll be your horse. Other people will ride her to keep her exercised and healthy, but if you want her, she's yours."

Cassidy hugged Chris tightly, burying her nose in his chest to hide the tears that were threatening to tumble down her cheeks. Instead, she breathed deeply, the scent of Chris searing itself into her brain as she squeezed him tighter.

"You're a dream, Chris Davis," she finally said. "Seriously, what girl wouldn't be charmed by an offer of a pony of her own?"

Noche snorted as if to say *I'm no pony*, and they both laughed. Walking back to the house, they were hand in hand, and when everyone gathered around for lunch, Cassidy felt at home on the big screened-in porch with the rest of the house.

Except for one thing.

"Y'all, I'm the only girl here," she noted as she passed a plate of fresh corn on the cob to her left to Dylan. He was blockier than his brothers, more of a college-aged muscle hunk than the leaner, slightly taller Chris. "You boys been busy?"

Brian laughed, spooning fruit salad into a bowl for himself. It was too hot for kitchen-prepared foods, so lunch was mostly cut-up fruits and vegetables, along with huge corned beef pastrami sandwiches piled on top of dark rye bread. Simple but honest and tasty.

"I think we've all sort of been keeping our heads down. No time for any fooling around," Brian said. "When Chris and Simon said they had this idea for a video game, we all jumped in, but we had no idea how much work it'd be to get *Sky Adventures* launched. And then there was learning how to run a company. I mean... I guess you understand, right?"

Cassidy blinked, part of her shocked. Was he making fun of her? But as she looked at Brian, she saw that he was being honest. He wasn't making fun of her or looking down on her experiences. To Brian Davis, Cassidy's work at her family's B&B was just as worthy as their billion-dollar video game company.

"I ... Thank you, Brian," she said. "I hadn't thought of it that way. Still, you boys better be careful, or else every single girl from here to Austin is going to be putting the Cloud 9 ranch in their phone maps."

Dylan grinned. "If they're all as pretty as you, Miss Cassidy, let 'em. I'll happily give any pretty lady who wishes a free horseback riding lesson."

"Except on Noche," Chris said. "She's Cassidy's."

Cassidy expected argument from the other brothers, but nobody said anything. Even Matt Miller just crunched on his sandwich, wiping a blob of mayonnaise from the corner of his mouth. Instead, everyone just took the declaration in stride until Matt chuckled. "Dylan, first *you* need to get good enough to give horseback riding lessons."

"I'm better than you!" Dylan said, and everyone laughed. "What? I am!"

"That's because I'm from San Diego, you doofus. I didn't even see a live horse until I was thirteen years old," Matt said good-naturedly. Seeing Cassidy's expression, he chuckled. "Didn't expect a California boy to be hanging out with these country bumpkins?"

"I didn't expect to find a California boy trying to live in Texas at all," Cassidy said. "But now that you're here, besides helping out with volleyball, what do you think you want to do?"

Matt schooled his features and gave Cassidy a nod. "Sell propane. And propane accessories."

Cassidy kept her stony face until first Andrew, and then Chris, cracked laughing. She joined in, and soon the entire porch was filled with laughter, pure and happy. She felt at home. She felt accepted, and she felt like she knew these men. They were all good men, men who'd worked hard and to this point either hadn't found the right person or the time to have love.

"You know, the football game's going to be more serious than you boys are prepared for," she said as she helped clear the table. Dylan had drawn washing-up duty and was already running a sink of water to wipe the dishes down. "I already told Chris how Carl's probably going to tape up his ankle and get out there."

"From what I've heard of Carl, I want to see it," Andrew said. "Tim too. But for everyone's sake, I think I might tweak the team division system to make sure the Norton brothers are on opposite teams."

"You sure the stadium's sturdy enough to handle that?" Chris asked with a wry little grin. "You know how brothers like to fight each other. Twin brothers? Could be worse."

"Nah, it's all in good fun," Cassidy said. "They won't do anything that'll require a hospital trip ... on purpose."

After lunch she and Chris went for a walk, holding hands as they went around the lake. "You have a good family."

"So do you," Chris said. "So when our mom comes to visit, I suppose you won't mind if she does what mothers do?"

"You mean ask me a bunch of questions that she thinks are sly but are about as pointed as a sword?" Cassidy asked. "Questions that all seem to focus on weddings and babies and such?"

Chris chuckled. "Yeah. I mean, I don't think Mom's like that, but I don't know, honestly. But I do want you two to get to know each other."

Cassidy gave Chris's hand a squeeze. "I'd like that too. Another thing I'd like, now that summer's here. Think we can go swimming?"

"The bottom's a little muddy, but I bet if I get Dylan and Matt on it, they'll figure out a nice little dock," Chris said. "Matt studied engineering in school; might as well put all that book learning to use somehow. But I've got a question."

"Shoot."

"What sort of swimsuit are we talking about?" Chris asked. "You know, for research purposes."

Cassidy laughed. "Well, it's been a while since I got to really swim, but I do believe I've got this little green triangle-top bikini that I bought during my time in juco. I should still be able to squeeze what I've got into it, if you'd like?"

Chris groaned and stopped, and Cassidy grinned. She knew what she was doing, and while they were being nice, that didn't mean she couldn't toss a handful of sass and spice in every once in a while.

After all, when she and Chris got to that stage when nice could be set aside, she wanted him to know that she had plenty of spice inside her. And when the time was right, she and he would be able to be as sweet or spicy as they both wanted.

"You're enjoying this," Chris said, and Cassidy walked on, swinging her hips from side to side as she did. She knew he was watching, and she wanted him to watch.

"Come on, dude." She waved him forward. "Let's keep walking, and then when I know your brothers can't be spying on us, you and I can have some private time."

"Do believe I like that," Chris said. "Some motivation for the game?"

Cassidy grinned. "Maybe. But just *some* motivation, right?"

"Definitely." Chris caught up and took her hand again. "You know, I don't play games."

"Good, because neither do I," Cassidy said. "Don't mean it won't be fun, though."

"That's for sure."

CHAPTER 17

The sky was bright blue, and as the afternoon sunlight glimmered off the rows of bleachers, Chris could feel sweat start to trickle down his chest. It was now summer in Saint Cloud, and the weather was ... well, Texas.

Thankfully, they'd prepared and had lots of drinks available. Andrew had gone all out for the game, with multiple flat packs of sports drinks stacked on the sidelines along with gallons of cold, cold water.

Chris knew there were at least a few bottles of beer stashed in people's cars and trucks too, but that was for the postgame celebration.

"Feeling good?" Chris asked Jenae as she stretched out, her pink hair ironically matching with the red jersey she was wearing.

"QaQ jajvam," Jenae, a certified Trekkie, said with a smirk. "It's a good day to die."

She flexed her biceps, where she had a tattoo with the Klingon symbol on it, and Chris chuckled. "Just remember not everyone speaks Klingon, so keep it to English when you're calling out to teammates."

"Yeah, but that means they understand my trash talk too," Jenae said. "What's the fun in that?"

Chris moved on, and in the middle of the field he saw Andrew shaking hands with Sheriff Monk, who wasn't dressed for the game but instead wore black athletic pants and a striped referee's shirt, and a tough-looking woman who was dressed to play. Andrew wasn't playing either, having agreed to work the sidelines instead as just a coach for Chris's team. "Hey, everyone ready?"

"Sure," Andrew said. "Chris, you know Sheriff Monk. He said he'll referee the game, and this is Chief Bronson of the fire department."

"A pleasure, Chief." Chris shook hands with the woman. "No offense, I hope to never see you in a professional capacity at the ranch."

Chief Bronson gave a flinty smile. "I hope so too, Mr. Davis. Your brother and I were just discussing the team rosters. I was sort of hoping to swap one of my guys for one of yours."

"Sorry, Chief. I'm not giving you Tim Norton," Andrew said with a grin. "I might be new in town, but I wasn't born yesterday."

Sheriff Monk laughed and shook his head. "Told you, Irene. Man's smart."

"Yup. Well, then, might as well flip the coin. Let's kick this off."

Chris's team won the flip, and he turned around to jog back to his sideline when he stopped, stunned.

It was Cassidy. Her long hair was pulled up into a ponytail, and she wore a black jersey like he was, her black shorts underneath showing him a long length of beautiful leg. He hurried over, amazed. "I didn't think you were playing."

"Please," she scoffed, smirking. "My brothers aren't the only Nortons who know how to play. I just didn't play for the team, but who do you think taught them how to cover the deep routes?"

"Until we turned eleven," Tim said as he came up, grinning. "So who's getting the ball first?"

"We are." Chris looked across the field as Brian and Dylan chatted up the red team. "We ready for this?"

"It's all fun," Tim reminded Chris, and for the first few minutes of the game, Chris thought Tim was right. The first kickoff punt and subsequent drive were all in fun, with lots of laughter and good play on all sides.

That all soured when one of the local Saint Cloud boys, Gavin Shaw, tagged Takeshi a bit hard, and Takeshi went tumbling. He took the fall well, rolling over his shoulder, but Chris could see that he wasn't pleased with it.

"You got something to say, newbie?" Gavin taunted. "Be glad we ain't got the helmets and pads out!"

"Where I come from, lad, we don't *need* pads," Hamish replied, the big man's jaw tightening. Chris pulled him back before he and Gavin could get into it, and the game continued.

But as plays turned into drives, tensions rose. Chris and Andrew started moving players on and off the field not because of wanting to have the best team out there, or even to have fun, but to keep a lid on tensions.

But even he could feel his nerves fraying. "Come on!" he yelled at one point when one of the ranch hands from the Bar-X threw a tight elbow to his lower back that jolted him out of the way of a pass. "What was that garbage?"

"Garbage?" the ranch hand growled. "What do you mean, dude? You gotta harden up!"

"Who're you calling dude, Robarts?" one of Chris's teammates yelled, getting in his face. "We work just as hard—"

Sheriff Monk blew his whistle, getting in between the two. "That's enough! Don't make me start throwing flags!"

Chris and the other player rotated out of the game, and on the sidelines, Chris grabbed a drink. "What was that?"

"Don't sweat it, new blood." Robarts glared across the field. "He's Bar-X, I'm Happy W. Those boys sometimes need reminding that just because I look good and smile for the customers don't mean I don't work just as hard as they do. And … hey!"

Out on the field, Cassidy was on the ground, holding her ankle. Above her stood another woman, a local who had a sneer on her face. Players on both sides were pushing and shoving, and Chris ran out onto the field, his eyes only for Cassidy.

"Cass?" he asked, kneeling next to her. "You okay?"

"Stay on the sidelines next time, booty queen," the other woman sneered. "You look comfortable on your knees, though."

"Hey!" Chris yelled, anger filling him. "You've got no right to—"

"Oh shut up, outsider!" someone yelled, and the argument was on. Chris couldn't tell who was what. Outsiders versus locals, ranch versus ranch, Chris couldn't tell what was triggering all of the fights.

But yelling escalated to pushing, and Sheriff Monk's whistle was ignored. Pushing got rougher, and suddenly a yell echoed through the stadium as a punch was thrown, and it was on.

Chris didn't care. He cared about Cassidy and turned his back to the melee, helping her to her feet. "You okay?"

"Yea—watch out!"

Chris turned, but before he could see what had caused Cassidy to yell, a human missile came hurtling in front of him as Carl Norton leveled one of his own teammates with a primal roar of dominance and a shoulder check that sent him flying. "You don't *touch* my sister!"

Madness. It was madness. Chris kept Cassidy next to him, and time seemed to slow down. He saw Jenae riding on the back of a local man, her tiny hand pummeling his head and neck. Takeshi was down, rolling back and forth with another man as Peter tried to separate them. Hamish and the man who'd knocked Chris down earlier were nose to nose, swinging haymakers at each other like a pair of drunken barbarians, blood already pouring down their faces.

"Come on, let's get you out of here," Chris said to Cassidy. But before they could move, a man tackled Carl, and Chris was pulled into the fray. He didn't even know the man. He was just a local, but he'd tried to hurt Carl. And Carl was Cassidy's brother, so it was with every ounce of strength inside him that he pistoned his fist forward and into the man's cheek and eye. Pain flared in his hand, but he didn't care.

What mattered was Cassidy. And family. He looked for his brothers, but they were safe, Brian and Dylan watching each other's backs. Chris looked for Tim, Simon, and Matt Miller, but in the chaos he could see none of the men.

Suddenly cold water started raining down on the field, and a siren wailed. The combination broke up most of the fighting, and everyone stopped a few seconds later when three shots cracked over the stadium, causing a few screams of surprise and terror. The sheriff did have a gun handy after all.

"Y'all cut that out before my deputies arrive and handcuffs start coming out," Sheriff Monk called, and Chris looked over to see him standing on top of a fire truck, Chief Bronson next to him with a dripping firehose in her hands. "This ain't Schneider versus Saint Cloud; y'all are adults."

People stopped, but as Chris looked around, he could see bodies still laid out on the ground. Some were making noise, groaning, or holding something.

But some weren't ... which scared him more.

CHAPTER 18

"How's the hand?" Cassidy asked Chris as he sat in the dining room, a washcloth pressed against his lip. She'd seen when he'd gotten punched, but he hadn't even noticed it. She should have been upset, but she wasn't. He'd taken that punch trying to help her, and to help Carl.

"I'll be okay." Chris barely glanced at his right hand. There was a bag of frozen peas there, resting on top of the knuckles and slowly thawing. Cassidy knew it could have been worse. When Chris had caught Duane Fickett, he'd caught him in the eye and cheek, not on one of the harder spots.

And Cassidy knew Duane had a hard head. He'd once head-butted a hole in the wall of Saint Cloud High's science lab, or at least that's what she'd heard.

"I'm sorry," Cassidy said quietly, sitting down. "I knew Arianna was on the other team, and I should have kept my distance."

"Who is she?" Chris asked, and Cassidy looked down, ashamed. "Cassidy?"

"She's someone who was hurt by my mistakes," Cassidy said quietly. "I told you, Chris, I'm not innocent. Couple years ago, I started dating who I *thought* was her ex-boyfriend. Except he hadn't told her they were exes yet."

She expected Chris to be repulsed, to be angry. Instead, he looked up at her with understanding and trust. "Does she know that you didn't know?"

"We … talked," Cassidy said. "Much like today's talks."

"I see." Chris took a deep breath. "This isn't your fault. If anything, it's on my brothers and I. We should have found a … a less physical way to try and get our people to form bonds with the community." He cleared his throat and stood up. "I'm going to go check on my people here, then go to the hospital. Hopefully, Peter's only banged up and not … concussed."

He left, and Cassidy felt an ache in her heart. He was shouldering the blame, probably more than his brothers were. After all, it was Chris and Simon who came up with the idea for the football game.

But the thing to Cassidy was, they'd tried. They'd walked into a minefield, not knowing that the careful balance of tensions that laced through any small city, including Saint Cloud, was going to be so disrupted.

That wasn't on Chris or the Davises. That was on Saint Cloud, and she needed to do something about it.

"Tim!" she hollered, standing up. Tim came out of the kitchen, where he'd been filling every container he could with water to make ice for the lumps and bruises that were filling the bed and breakfast. "I need to get changed to go out."

"What for?" Tim asked, trying to lift his eyebrow and failing. He'd taken a few shots himself, old high school rivals who figured they could get a sucker punch in on the former terror of Schneider High's football team. As such, his right eye was a little puffy, and he was probably going to be sporting a shiner the next day. "We could use someone to run to the drug store, lot of sprained ankles and wrists."

"I'll swing by on my way back if it's not an emergency," Cassidy said. "I've got something more important to deal with."

Quickly, Cassidy went to her room and sent a text message to Amelia Hernandez. *We need to talk about what happened at the football game ASAP.*

That done, she then changed from her sweaty and stained shorts and T-shirt into jeans and one of her better blouses. Running a brush through her hair, she put it down when her phone buzzed, and she saw it was from Amelia. *City Hall as quick as you can?*

Ten minutes.

It was actually seven—Cassidy pushed her truck a little faster than she should have and got lucky with a couple of green lights. Parking in front of City Hall, she saw Chief Bronson directing a trio of firefighters, all of whom were still wearing their football game clothes, in hand waxing the same truck she'd had to use to break up the fight.

Cassidy had to give her credit. While using fire hoses to break up a potential riot might have had problematic historical issues, she'd done it right, not attacking anyone but merely wetting everyone down to try and splash some sense into the mob.

Cassidy hurried up the stairs and into City Hall, where she found Amelia sitting in her office wearing probably the least professional outfit she'd ever seen her in, a pair of pink Lycra exercise shorts and a T-shirt with the deceased pro wrestler Eddie Guerrero on it. He might have been from El Paso and not Saint Cloud, but he was a Texas legend.

"Cassidy, to say my afternoon's been a mess is an understatement," Amelia said by way of greeting. "I was doing my best on a Peloton course when Billie Vincent comes knocking on my door telling me that your boyfriend and the folks staying at your place started a brawl at the football game. And here I was feeling bad for reluctantly passing since I can't catch a ball."

"I don't know, it might have been nice to see you scrap out there," Cassidy said with a soft smile. "I know how you are when someone makes you take off your hoops."

Amelia, who was famous professionally for her hooped earrings, didn't laugh even if her face did soften some. "So what happened?"

"We happened," Cassidy said simply. "Amelia, you know how this town is. Yeah, we might smile, shake hands, all of that. But there's divisions in this town. We know how to navigate those divisions, when to reach across the aisle and when to leave well enough alone. The Davis brothers don't. And that's on us, on me. It should be on Steve Monk for not keeping a sharper eye on the players, knowing that a ranch hand from the Happy W and a ranch hand from the Bar-X might get chippy at the drop of a hat."

"So what do you want to do about it?" Amelia asked. "I'll tell you, Tom's in his office, getting an earful from Kim Johnson right now. So you better have something good to say. Me, I'm on your side if only for the money reasons. The Davis brothers are investing in Dusty Bend, and I want my district to grow beyond wine money."

"Then let's go talk to them," Cassidy said. "If you don't mind?"

Amelia looked at her shorts and shrugged. "Tom Jones has seen me in worse. Come on."

They went next door, where Amelia walked into the mayor's office without even knocking. Cassidy saw that Kimberly Johnson was there, dressed professionally already, while Tom was in what could best be described as Saint Cloud business casual, khakis and a golf shirt. "Amelia—"

"Nope, Kim, you've been saying your piece to Tom here for what, twenty minutes?" Amelia said. "Tom's got a duty to listen to both sides and both of us. I'm just letting Cassidy here say what she has to say."

Kimberly opened her mouth for a moment, then closed it. "Fine. I was just telling the mayor that today's mess is a sign of the problems that the Davis brothers and their *video game* studio are going to bring to town. Now, I'm all about giving them their rights, and if they want to buy property, that's fine. But we shouldn't be rolling out the red carpet for these people."

"Oh, put a sock in it, Kimberly," Cassidy growled. "These people? Do you even hear yourself? What sort of closed-minded stereotype *crap* is that?"

"I—"

"Hold on, Kim." Tom lifted a hand. "I think Cassidy here might have a unique insight on all of this. And not just because of your ... close relationship with Chris Davis."

"Does everyone know we're dating?" Cassidy asked, rolling her eyes when everyone in the room nodded. "This town's one big Facebook group. Fine. Yes, Chris and I are dating. But that's not what I'm talking about. The Davis brothers are just about half an accent and six months of savvy away from fitting right in with Saint Cloud natives. I'm talking about the other folks they have here. They've been living with me in my bed and breakfast for just about two weeks now, and here's what I've learned. They're weird. They're different. I can still barely understand the big one, Hamish, because of his Scottish accent. But you know what? They're good people. They're good people who work hard. And maybe we don't get their work, all that pounding on a keyboard they do. But they work hard. I see their faces when they come back from work and look like zombies. I see their faces in the morning, when they eat their breakfasts and have to cobble together the same scraps of courage and drive and energy that the rest of us do when faced with another day of work that maybe we like but still gets tiring. It's the same look I see in the mirror most mornings."

"They're going to *change* Saint Cloud, Cassidy," Kimberly said. "A thousand or more new people? That's five percent of town."

"Worried about your next election, Kimberly?" Cassidy asked harshly. "Five percent's a big swing, you know."

"No."

"Then think of this. When our grandparents were kids, Saint Cloud had a huge change then too. Kimberly's Northside

District was nothing but shacks and trailer parks back then, or part of the Lazy Q ranch. Then World War II happened, and all those boys who'd gone off to war came back with GI Bill benefits and VA loans ... and the Northside became what it is today. I bet if we went back to about 1947 or so, there'd be y'all's predecessors arguing about how those neighborhoods were changing Saint Cloud."

"Never mind who was and who wasn't allowed in the Northside back then," Amelia held up a hand. "Sorry, discussion for another time."

"Thank you, Amelia. I'm not trying to fight *all* the culture wars today," Tom said tiredly. "So what are you advocating, Cassidy? That we open our arms wide and let the Davis brothers and their people just do whatever they want in town?"

"Would that be that bad, as long as they don't break the law?" Cassidy asked. "Tom, the other day, I had one of those chia-hemp seed organic bagels that the coders bought online because that's what they want to eat. Guess what? It was good with a little butter on it. So who cares if they want to eat different things, if they want to dye their hair pink or wear spangly suspenders? That'll mean new business opportunities in town."

"Great... Hippie Mart," Kimberly grumbled but sighed. "Still, that doesn't mean we roll out the red carpet for 'em."

"The Davis brothers don't need a red carpet, Kimberly. Those boys can *buy* the red carpet if they want to," Cassidy pointed out. "But too often around Saint Cloud, we say we're not going to roll out the red carpet when what we really do is put out an icy shoulder."

"So what do you suggest?" Tom asked. "I'm obviously not going to tell Steve Monk to run the newcomers out of town. That's not our way."

"No, but maybe we can open our arms and say welcome a bit better than we have," Cassidy said. "Look, the Davis brothers have offered up their barn to restart the barn dance tradition again, right?"

"That hasn't been decided yet," Tom pointed out. "The Davises might be offering up their barn, but that's community resources being used for the event."

Cassidy pursed her lips, not wanting to argue with Tom that the city bringing over some speakers and the sound system used by the high schools or the county fair for their outdoor events was hardly a great expenditure of community resources. They already had the speakers, and she was sure the barn could support the electricity draw. "Tom, I'm just saying that they deserve another chance. Like Chris told me before he went to check on his injured people, he should have thought of a way that wasn't so … physically violent."

"Could have been worse," Amelia pointed out with a small laugh. "Imagine if they'd decided to join in on the county fair Toughman boxing?"

Everyone could laugh about that a bit, and Cassidy felt the tension in the room drop a few degrees. "Tom, Kim, we can all agree to disagree civilly. But on this, I think it's important that you agree with me. This town can be better *with* the Cloud 9 crew than without them. Not just because of the money, either. Although that'll be nice. But because they're good people."

She stood back, her face flushed after what was probably the longest spiel she'd made in a long time. In fact, the last time she'd spoken so vehemently to anyone other than her family was back in junior college in a debate class.

So she was surprised when Kimberly, who'd seemed to be totally against any idea at first, nodded and hummed. "Maybe you're right, Cassidy. I'm not saying that I'm fully on your side, but maybe giving these folks another chance isn't too bad either. I mean, it's a barn dance. What's the worst that can happen?"

"Barn burns down and a hundred people die in a scene out of *Mad Max*?" Tom asked, then chuckled. "Amelia, your opinion?"

Amelia looked across the room at Kimberly and snorted in amusement. "I think this might be the first time in months that Kimberly and I are on the same side of an issue," she said. "I think we should throw our full support behind the barn dance. I'll even make sure to attend, if only to see if Kimberly can dance as well as that goody-two-shoes country girl image of hers puts off."

"Oh, I can dance circles around you, Amelia," Kimberly said. "What about you?"

"I can dance circles around you in country *and* Latin music." Amelia rolled her shoulders and grinned. "Speaking of which, think we can get some Latin music for the dance?"

"I'm down if you're down," Kimberly said. "And my partner's going to be cuter than yours."

"Ladies, ladies!" Tom declared as Cassidy tried not to laugh at the feminine rivalry being displayed before her eyes. "There's still a decision to be made, and to be honest, I'm not sure. I need some time to think, and the way I'm thinking now, we can all decide on Friday during the city council meeting. The community will be able to comment then, and we'll vote on it. Agreed?"

Kimberly and Amelia nodded, still looking at each other with challenging eyes. "Agreed. Better have your dancing boots ready, Kim," Amelia said. "I'll be taking off my hoops for this dance."

"Bring it, Dawn Quixote," Kimberly said, smiling. "These boots are made for walking, and … you know how it goes."

Cassidy cleared her throat. "Okay, all, we've had enough for today, haven't we? And you two are on the same side here, remember?"

Amelia nodded, and took a step back. "Right, Cassidy. Come on, I'll walk you out. Thanks for coming by."

CHAPTER 19

When Cassidy had told Chris and his brothers about her meeting with Amelia Hernandez and the other members of the city government, Chris had at first been upset. While he knew that Cassidy's heart was in the right place, the fact that she'd gone to Amelia Hernandez without even telling him was ... annoying.

The fight was his mistake; he didn't need Cassidy to fix things. But after thinking about it for a little bit, he realized that she'd done what she'd done out of the goodness of her heart. A single lunch together had confirmed it, and now, as the city council meeting approached, he chuckled. Adjusting his tie, he looked in the mirror to see Dylan leaning in the doorway. "How do I look?"

"Stupid," Dylan replied good-naturedly. "Good heavens, Chris, it's still ninety degrees outside, and you're dressing like you're in a Quentin Tarantino movie."

"What can I say?" Chris adjusted his tie. "I don't exactly have a lot of suits."

Dylan shook his head, chuckling. "Yeah, well, you might want to pick up another one or two in colors besides black, bro. Seriously, the sci-fi MIB look is very limiting."

"What do you suggest, a bolo tie, calfskin sport coat, and a Stetson?" Chris asked. "I still feel like a fake with my hat on when I ride the horses."

"How about we start with gray, and maybe something navy blue?" Dylan said. "After tonight's meeting. Sorry I can't go."

"Meh, don't worry about it." Chris clapped Dylan on the shoulder. "It's funny, really. You didn't pick up a scratch during the game or the fight, but you had to go and sprain your ankle the day afterwards."

"Yeah … in my retelling of the story, I'll probably omit saying I did that walking down the steps of the house," Dylan admitted with a small laugh. "So are you worried about tonight? I've been hearing that this has become a big issue in town."

"I'm sure it's just a tempest in a teapot," Chris said, although he was worried. He'd heard the same things, and if anything, more townspeople were suspicious of the coders and the Davises than before. While Andrew had patched things over with Justin Logan and Amanda Munoz, there was still tension with the neighbors.

Andrew and Brian were waiting for him when he came downstairs, and they shared a ride in the SUV into town. Chris's worry rose when he saw that the City Hall parking lot was already full.

"If they're carrying pitchforks when we walk in," Chris said, "I'm running."

"Only after we push Brian into the middle of them," Andrew joked.

"Jerk."

"I'm just saying you could tame a mob, that's all," Andrew said innocently as they climbed the steps.

They got to the council chambers, which was packed, but as Chris looked around, he saw Cassidy up front, with Carl and Tim, wide-stanced, squatting on multiple chairs. Nobody was willing to cross the Norton brothers over them, and Chris was able to sit down next to Cassidy, who looked him over. "You're handsome tonight."

"Thanks," he said, taking her hand. "You look beautiful."

Cassidy, who was wearing a blue, thigh-length cotton dress, looked down. "This old thing? I just threw it on."

"Uh-huh."

Tom Jones banged a gavel from his seat, and the crowd quieted. "Okay, folks, glad to see you decided to test the new air conditioner," he said with a touch of homely humor. "I'm not going to dance around for you. I know most of you are here for one subject. I can read the *Independent* as well as anyone, and I've even checked out a Facebook post or two."

Chris gave Cassidy's hand a squeeze, and she squeezed back. He'd read the editorial in the most recent edition of the *Saint Cloud Independent*, the twice-weekly local newspaper that usually confined itself to ads, announcements of church bake sales, and coverage of local school news. Their editorial style was mostly down-home cheerleading more than anything else.

Until the most recent edition, where the editor had devoted a whole half page to blasting the fight and the "outside agitators" who'd apparently caused it. According to the *Independent*, every punch, every broken tooth, every bruise or injury was a direct result of the Davis brothers and their merry band of video game misfits.

Somehow they even mined characters from *Sky Adventures* to make allusions, such as the fact that Lionna, one of the female characters that could join a player's party, was drawn with an enhanced figure. Never mind that Lionna wore a full-steel breastplate and long leather trousers. Because of the curves of her armor, she was obviously an "unwholesome influence."

Chris was only glad that the editor didn't dig deeper into the story or the various options that he'd allowed the programmers to put into character choices. While nobody crossed a line that he was uncomfortable with, he knew that even in modern times, having all sorts of characters in a game was seen as scandalous by some.

The assembly quieted down, and the mayor continued. "But, before we get to that matter, there are some normal business things that we've got to take care of. Starting with a report from Chief Bronson on this year's 'Fill The Boot' charity drive. Chief?"

For the next half hour, the council moved through routine business as quickly as possible, Mayor Jones gaveling things quickly so as to keep the crowd from becoming restless. Finally, he got to the crux of the night's meeting.

"Next order of business, the proposal for the city to support the re-start of the so-called barn dances to be held at the Cloud 9 ranch. To be clear, the Davis family has offered the city the use of the barn to hold community dances and other appropriate community events free of charge. However, the city would be using community equipment such as speakers, amplifiers, and such for the dances. Before the council hears from the community, I'd like to ask Andrew Davis, the oldest of the Davis brothers, if the barn's renovations are complete?"

Andrew got up, foregoing the microphone. "It is, Mayor. There is plenty of parking, too, long as you don't mind walking through some tall grass."

"Thank you, Mr. Davis," the mayor replied. "Now I'd like to open up the floor to community comment. Remember, y'all, while you might have feelings involved in this matter, keep it polite. This is a good town, with good people. So do your best to speak that way. Okay, who's first?"

Instead of a lectern or podium, the city council used a wireless microphone to allow the community to speak, and speak they did. For the next hour, people said their piece in two-minute spots before passing the microphone on to someone else.

"Now, I was born here in Saint Cloud," one man said, "and other than a few years where I took a little trip to Iraq with a man named Schwarzkopf, I've lived here in Saint Cloud all of my fifty-seven years. And let me tell you, I don't need or want no outside influences changing this town! I like knowing that when I go to the store, what I'll see is regular food. Real food. I like knowing my neighbors and knowing that even if we don't see eye to eye on everything, there's certain things we do agree on. Like the Cowboys."

A ripple of laughter rolled through the crowd, and the man continued. "Now, these new folks, they may be perfectly fine people. I'm sure there's a place for them that they can be comfortable, where they can get their sorts of things in their sorts of lifestyle. But Saint Cloud ain't it, and we for sure shouldn't be spending city money so as they can pretend that they're hunky-dory with us now!"

The argument continued, and Chris was shocked at the amount of vehemence on both sides of the issue. Another woman got up, looking around. "My family lives in Dusty Bend, and when I hear a lot of you talk about how we shouldn't be welcoming, you know what I hear? I hear the same things I heard when I was a little girl, and the kids living in the rich parts of town told a girl from the Bend that I wasn't welcome around these parts. I heard the kids with the new bikes taunting me for my bike from the church yard sale and how I was nothing more than a "Dusty Girl." It took me a long, long time to understand what that taunt meant. Now we've got new folks wanting to come in, bringing with them change and investment. Y'all ain't fooling nobody. You just want to keep on top of the pile here in Saint Cloud. But the Bend needs the jobs, the investment. So what if things change? Maybe when my daughter's called a 'Dusty Girl,' it'll mean something different then."

The argument went on and on, and Chris listened. But more importantly, he watched as the city council reacted to the comments.

"Amelia's on our side," Chris whispered to Brian, who was sitting next to him. "Kim Johnson?"

"She's on your side," Cassidy said, her eyes also looking at the council. "But Duane Cortez isn't sure. Your new presence doesn't do much for his district."

Chris looked where Cassidy was, thinking about what he knew about Duane Cortez. He represented the area around the Depot and the far eastern side of town and, as such, was usually more concerned with the businesses in the area than the residents. There just weren't that many, not compared to the other districts.

And while there were business opportunities for Duane's district, there were also dangers. After all, Chris's family and business didn't need agricultural supplies, and the car dealerships out there didn't exactly stock the sort of vehicles that most of the game studio's workers would want to drive.

"What about the other one, Vance Henry?" Brian asked Cassidy. "The man's got a poker face."

"He always does," Cassidy whispered back. "You need one vote, remember? That's all."

"Then you say something, Chris," Andrew said. "Listen to the people. The folks against us don't care about dollars and cents or jobs. They *feel*. Brian can't reach them, and I'm already the money guy. You can reach them."

Chris stopped, listening as people continued to talk. And he realized his brother was right. The people opposed to the barn dances, and more importantly to the Davises and the game studio, were arguing from a place of fear. Their world was threatening to change, and they didn't want that.

But change was coming ... It was just how he presented that change.

The mayor's eyes flickered to his group, and Chris stood up, taking the microphone. "Thank you. First, everyone, I'm Chris Davis, for those of you who don't know me. Simon Smith, who was born and raised here, my brothers and I, we're the guys who bought the Cloud 9, we're the guys who own the business a lot of you are talking about. And we're the guys who put together that … utter *disaster* of a football game last weekend."

There was light laughter, and Chris took a deep breath. "I've been sitting here for an hour or so now, listening. And I want you to know, on both sides of the issue, that I've heard you all. I've heard, and your words are right here to me." He tapped his chest. "And that's what I want to talk with you about.

"When my best friend Simon Smith told me about this great little town in Texas that would be a good place to build our new company headquarters, my first response was to check him for a fever. But he was stubborn … Saint Cloud stubborn. And when I got here, I learned what he meant."

Chris took a deep breath and looked around. "I'm not gonna lie to you people. I don't fully understand Saint Cloud yet. But I've learned this *is* a good town, with good people. Now, Simon, my brothers, and I, we do want to build our headquarters here, and yes, we'll be bringing in new people to fill the jobs that local folks can't. But those new people? I know most of them too. They're good people as well. And you know what they'll find, I hope? The same imperfect, stubborn, hotter than the backdoor of hell in summer … wonderful, kind, and special town that I've found. Yeah, it'll make change. But change isn't always a bad thing. New things, new faces … new people can change your life."

He looked at Cassidy, who was looking at him with big eyes. "Sometimes, new faces are what you've searched the whole world for. New faces that grab your heart and won't let go. New faces that you want to make family and who make you realize that no matter what, you're sticking. And that's what's happened to me. Saint Cloud's where I belong … where my heart belongs. So if you don't want to do the barn dance? Well, I have to admit, it's gonna sting some. But I plan on dancing in that barn in a couple weeks, dancing with someone very, very special to me. I hope you folks will be there to see me."

Silence reigned, and nobody spoke as Chris sat down, taking Cassidy's hand again, and she leaned in to kiss his cheek.

"I meant every word," he whispered to her. "I'd say more, but what I mean to say shouldn't be part of city council meeting notes."

Cassidy chuckled and leaned in, giving him another kiss. It was a tender, emotional kiss, and while it was a very chaste kiss, it meant more for what it told his heart.

She was his.

He was hers.

The rest of it was just … minor details.

Dimly, Chris heard a few "awws" from the crowd, and the mayor cleared his throat. "Well, now, I'm not going to say this is the first time someone's kissed in this room—after all, we do weddings here too," he said to more laughter, "but I think it's time to vote. Can I get a second?"

"I second, Mayor," Amelia Hernandez said. "On the motion to support the barn dance, how does the council vote?"

The mayor nodded. "District one, Councilwoman Johnson?"

"Aye. Support the dance."

"District two, Councilman Henry?"

The older man took off his round-rimmed glasses, and Chris could feel his chest tighten. He really was a good poker player until he set the glasses down and leaned forward. "For the dance. Yes."

At that point, it was anticlimactic. Of course Amelia voted for the motion, and seeing himself backed into a corner, Duane Cortez went along with it. The only thing left was for Tom to smile and pick up his gavel. "Well then, let's just make it unanimous. Five to zero, the motion carries."

The gavel dropped to the table, and Chris clapped. He wasn't the only one, and he felt good as he stopped to put an arm around Cassidy. "So, there's this dance coming up," he said in her ear. "I think I need a date."

Cassidy grinned. "I think I know a girl who might say yes."

"Is that so?" Chris asked, and Cassidy nodded. "Well, then, will you be my date to the dance, Cassidy?"

"As long as you promise to get me home by midnight," Cassidy teased. "After all, I've got a reputation to uphold."

CHAPTER 20

It took nearly all of the next two weeks to pull everything together in the end, which was perfect for the coders in Cassidy's eyes. They'd burned the midnight oil literally, everyone working almost around the clock to get the online update to *Sky Adventures* finished. It had been stressful, with Cassidy and Chris not being able to see a lot of each other. Even though the entire team was working through their lunch breaks to get the update done, they did manage two quick lunches together.

But that meant that tonight was a celebration of many sorts. The update was done; she knew that from the coders. They were eager for a break, and after tonight's festivities, they were all planning on being comatose for at least two days.

After that? Well, they were taking it one day at a time. Some had already booked appointments with real estate agents to see available houses or apartments in Saint Cloud. Others were taking their time, happy to stay at the Norton bed and breakfast until they were certain their future was in Saint Cloud.

Cassidy knew where her future lay. With her arm entwined through his, she walked toward the big barn, which was already so filled that a lot of folks were gathered in the freshly smoothed and cleaned dirt outside the big double doors, sipping on tea and sitting on hay bales.

"Don't tell me Tom Jones paid for hay bales and refreshments," Cassidy said, and Chris shook his head. "You guys?"

"We can afford it," Chris said simply. "And the beta testers and social media teams are already happy with the new update. We're going to be in a good place for the next game."

They got into the barn, where Chris stopped at her side, surprised. "Are they doing … the Carlton?" he asked, lifting an eyebrow. "And the music?"

"Told you, Tom Jones leans into his namesake," Cassidy said with a soft laugh. "Besides, you have to admit Matt Miller looks like he's having fun."

It was probably the strangest thing she'd seen in six months, the tall, lanky former basketball player in a bright white shirt and brand new bootcut jeans … and Jordan shoes, hamming it up with Saint Cloud's only female sheriff's deputy, Billie Vincent, who did her best to keep up with the tall man despite the massive difference in their heights. She looked very different from her work attire, her red hair flying around in a cloud as she danced in a gingham dress.

The song wrapped up and everyone clapped, especially Tom himself, who was leading the dance. The music changed to a more traditional country music theme, and Cassidy tapped her foot. "What do you think?"

"Still prefer rock for working out, but I've heard worse," Chris said with a chuckle. "Last year Hamish insisted on the entire coding team watching the Eurovision finals. That was painful."

Cassidy laughed. "You know, after a month with your crew? I'm looking forward to how things are going to change around Saint Cloud."

"Me too," Chris said, smiling a little. "But not too much."

"Like what?"

"Like that Mexican place just down the street from our temporary offices." Chris patted his stomach. "They've got to stay in business."

Cassidy laughed, nodding. "Don't worry, Tio Tito's isn't going anywhere."

The music changed again, and Chris tilted his head. "Would you dance with me, Cassidy?"

Cassidy took his hand, and as Allison Krause serenaded them, they danced slowly, his hands on her lower back and her hands around his neck. "It's been a tough two weeks, not having you around," she admitted softly. "This feels good."

"I know what you mean," Chris said quietly, tracing his fingers up her back. "Know what I've learned?"

"That you're a pretty good leader and public speaker?" Cassidy joked, and Chris smiled. "What have you learned?"

"That every word I said was true. My heart's here, Cassidy. With you. And I don't want to go two weeks again without you by my side. I know we might want to take our time on some stuff, but ... my mind's made up. I'm yours. I love you."

Cassidy had expected it to happen. She'd known for weeks how she felt about Chris. She knew that when she thought of her future, it was only with him by her side. But hearing him say it for the first time brought tears to her eyes, and she smiled up at him. "I love you too, Chris."

He pulled her close, and even if it wasn't typical barn dance behavior, she didn't care as his lips met hers, and they stopped dancing to kiss through the rest of the song. When the music stopped, Cassidy stayed where she was until she felt a tap on her shoulder and looked to see Carl there. "Mind if I cut in, Chris?"

"Of course." Chris stepped back. "Think I'll go grab a tea."

Cassidy took Carl's hand, and the two danced, Cassidy chuckling as memories came back. "Remember when I taught you how to do this?"

"Junior high dance, eighth grade," Carl said. "You were taller than me then."

"For about two months," Cassidy said with a laugh before sighing happily. "He said it, Carl."

Carl nodded, smiling back. "Good. Took the man long enough; everyone's known it for weeks. Did he pop the big question?"

"Not yet," Cassidy said. "It's way too early. Sounds weird to talk about that with my little brother."

"I just want you to be sure about him when he does."

"Keep it up, Carl," Cassidy teased. "People are going to start thinking you're a good guy again."

Carl snorted. "Doubtful. But we'll see."

Chris returned, and Cassidy felt like she was floating. With her hand in his, or his arm around her shoulder, she felt at home. Better yet, she saw people smiling, having fun.

She saw bridges being built.

Some of them were funny, like pink-haired Jenae dancing with one of the ranch hands from the Bar-X ranch to a Jason Aldean boot-slapper, neither of them in time with the music but both having fun messing up.

Or gigantic Hamish riding a hay bale like it was a bull, his whoops probably the most understandable thing most people in town had ever heard from him.

Some of them were sweet, like watching Takeshi subtly flirting with Marcy, Tom Jones' assistant. Or seeing the class presidents from Saint Cloud High and Schneider High share a glass of tea while giving each other looks.

But the highlight for Cassidy was the traditional square dance. Sheriff Monk was the caller, his little pot belly poking out his sequined shirt and making him look somehow more fit the role.

"Now I'm gonna go a little slow at first; some of y'all ain't square danced in a long time … Kimberly Johnson," the sheriff called, causing the whole barn to laugh. A fiddler started up, and Chris bowed to Cassidy, who bowed back.

"Shall we, my lady?"

"We shall, my good sir."

It didn't matter if they were following the calls perfectly or if their do-si-do was done without turning. It didn't matter that

Chris bumped into Amelia Hernandez as she and Dylan tried to dance as well, or that Cassidy stepped on Brian's toes.

What mattered was the sense of family. The smile on her face when she saw Carl dancing with Justin Logan's little sister, or the feeling inside her when the sheriff called out, "Now bow to your partner, and we're done!"

The thunderous applause that filled the barn overwhelmed everything but the beating of her heart, and as she turned to look at Chris, she knew that for the first time in a very, very long time … she was completely happy.

Holding hands, they left the barn, saying their goodbyes as quietly as they could. "Thank you, both of you," Amelia said at the door. "Now go be happy."

"I am happy," Cassidy replied, giving Amelia a hug. "Thank you for having coffee at my place."

Chris and Cassidy walked into the night, the relative coolness of the air kissing her sweaty skin. "I wasn't lying, you know," she said to Chris once they were alone. "I am happy."

"Me too," he replied. "There's a ton to do, and a lot of challenges in the future, but you know what? With you by my side, I'm ready for them."

"Good." Cassidy bit her lip and took a deep breath. "I want to go get on the horses, ride out into the fields alone with you."

Chris pulled her in close and lifted her in his arms. "Then let's go for a moonlight ride."

Thank you for reading Cloudy with a Chance of Cowboy.

You can dive right into Cloudy with a Chance of Billionaire… turn the page for a peek-a-book.

CHAPTER 21

"They should have done this last week." Brian adjusted his bowtie. Next to him, his friend Simon ran a brush around the toe of his boots, which made Brian chuckle inside. The wedding ceremony was over, and they were going to the big barn on the ranch for the reception. No matter what, they were going to be walking through dust and dirt.

"Why's that?" Simon asked, putting the brush down. They were sharing a room since Cassidy Davis—as of an hour ago, Cassidy Norton—had claimed Simon's room as her changing area. While she'd made a gorgeous bride in her elegant white wedding dress with a big hoop skirt and seven-foot train, there was no way she was going to wear that thing for a reception in the Cloud 9 Ranch's barn.

Weddings on private property were a juggling act of compromises.

"They would have been able to do a costume-themed wedding that way, matching up with Halloween," Brian explained. "I mean, the ceremony was nice, but doing a whole *Corpse Bride* thing would have been great. And the reception could have been a trick-or-treat."

"Brian, you'd better not be calling my sister a trick," Carl Norton's eyes flashed with warning from across the room. He'd just pulled his tuxedo jacket back on, and Brian could see that his offhand comment had put the man on edge.

"Relax, Carl." Brian wasn't afraid of the former All-State linebacker, the man known at one time for having the shortest fuse in Saint Cloud. But at the same time, the man had become his brother-in-law within the last hour. No reason to spoil a Texas wedding with a Texas-sized family feud. "If anything, Cassidy's a treat. I'm doing backflips over the class she's bringing to our family. Now, how Chris tricked her into accepting his proposal, I won't ever know. But that's on your sister to figure that out."

Carl considered Brian's words, then laughed. "Yeah, guess so. I'm going to go find Tim, see if he's found that big cup of coffee he was looking for."

Carl left the room, and Brian waited until the door was closed before looking over at Simon. "Does he realize how easy he makes the jokes sometimes?"

"Remember," Simon chuckled. "Carl's probably never been to Canada. And Tim can't help his name."

"Still … Tim Norton and coffee…" Brian laughed. He finished redoing his tie and looked over at Simon. "Changing subjects, you're going single today."

Simon nodded, shrugging. "I would have loved to bring a special someone, but that wasn't in the cards."

"I understand." Brian glanced out the window, seeing movement around the barn.

"So … when is it going to be you headin' into the barn?" Simon asked.

Brian shrugged. "Come on, man. You know me."

"Oh, I do. Brian Davis, the boy who literally dated his way through the cheerleading team during his junior year of college. You were still a legend on campus when Chris and I went. Lonely, dateless nerds all over campus had secret shrines to you, offering sacrifices in order to absorb at least a little of your swagger."

Brian shook his head. "That was long ago, man. Honestly? Don't know if I'll ever settle down. Not that I'm opposed to it, I know my rep, but … well, any woman who's going to put up with me and my garbage has to be so hardheaded that we'd end up fighting as much as anything else."

"Yeah, she'd have to crack the whip for sure. And don't sweat your rep any longer, man. I mean seriously, it's been what, years since you and—"

"Don't say her name," Brian interjected, a little heatedly. It might have been years for everyone else, but hearing that name made it feel like it was yesterday to him.

"I'm just saying …" Simon came over, "you're not the playboy you were in college. Haven't been for a long time. What you need to do is forgive her … and forgive yourself."

"Myself?" Brian asked. Simon nodded. "For what?"

"For letting your heart lead you more than your head. That's not a bad thing. Now, as for the future Mrs. Brian Davis?

Yeah, she'll have to be hardheaded, but I'll let you in on a secret."

"What's that?"

Simon leaned in, clapping Brian on the shoulder. "Saint Cloud's got *a lot* of hardheaded women. Come on, before they say we're holding up the show."

Brian nodded, and they left his room to go to the barn for the reception. It was bigger than the ceremony itself, which had been open to only a dozen people in total. But the Nortons were almost minor celebrities in town, and the Davises were … Well, they could count themselves amongst the "big hats" in Saint Cloud. So as Brian entered the barn, he slipped into the comfortable role he'd sculpted for himself over the years. After all, his job was public relations, and so it was with practiced ease that he started smiling, shaking hands.

"Amanda," he greeted, smiling. Looking the woman up and down, his smile grew. "A dress? This is a special occasion!"

Amanda Munoz, the owner of the neighboring Happy W dude ranch, waved him off with a laugh. "I had to prove that they actually exist. Congratulations."

"Thank you. The house is going to be a lot quieter," Brian quipped, making Amanda laugh again in understanding. "I'll be honest, the big house is emptying out faster than I thought."

"True, but I'm watching them build your brother's new house from the top of the ridge," said Amanda, who was renting a huge chunk of the Cloud 9's land. "Cassidy's going to be a very happy woman. Plenty of room for young 'uns, from the looks of things."

Brian laughed. "Don't tell Chris that. He'll faint!"

Amanda grinned, shaking her head. "Call me old fashioned, but isn't that what honeymoons are for? I know, I know, I'm a generation behind, but when I was up there on my horse watching them work on the house, in my mind I could see three or four little Davis boys and girls running around that big space."

Brian laughed softly. "I'd like that. We'd build them a proper swing set and play equipment, too. None of that plastic garbage they make now."

"For sure," Amanda said. "Well, enjoy."

Amanda moved on, and Brian did the same, doing what he knew was expected of him. Wedding receptions were the sort of gathering that could help his family with their position in Saint Cloud's social hierarchy. Instead of just being the "new rich boys," it was a chance to forge the bonds that could make them a true part of the community.

When Chris and Cassidy entered, the reception really got started, and Brian had a good time. But as the dancing continued, he hung back, not joining in. Instead, he sat at his table, sipping a flute of Champagne and watching as Chris and Cassidy had their first dance as husband and wife.

Did he want that? Sure. But like he told Simon, finding a woman who could put up with him would be like finding a golden needle in a barn-sized haystack.

The first dance ended, and Brian got up from his chair not to dance but to pay his respects to Mayor Tom Jones, who'd been kind enough to "lend" the same sound equipment the city used for the community barn dances at the ranch for the reception. "Well, Mayor, what do you think?"

"I think y'all gonna have to step up your barn dance game come next spring," the mayor laughed. "You set a mighty high bar here with this shindig, Brian."

Brian laughed, shrugging. "Can you blame us?"

"Not at all, young man … Well, hello there, Mrs. Davis."

Brian turned, expecting to see his mother, who'd flown in for the wedding. Instead, he was surprised to see Cassidy, looking gorgeous in her ice-blue reception dress. "Cassidy."

"I promised your mother that I would dance with all of her sons at this reception," Cassidy smiled, "and I've got my brothers too. I was going to start with Andrew, you know, work from oldest on down, but your mother's claimed him, and Tim made me promise to do the Chicken Dance when it's his turn. So what do you say?"

Brian tilted his head, nodding as he heard the music, grinning. "I suppose I can dance to The B-52s with you. It's one of Mom's faves."

Brian took Cassidy by the hand, and moments later they were shaking their bodies, acting foolish, and laughing their heads off. Andrew and their mother were right there with them, turning it into sort of a four-person boogie that had Brian grinning.

"Now, Mom, you're going to have to apologize to Andrew," Cassidy said as the song ended and she clapped. "This barn might be a bit dilapidated, but it's no *shack*."

"Oh, you're going to be just what these boys need." Mrs. Davis gave them affectionate pats. "I'm so looking forward to visiting for Christmas."

"Us too, Mom," Andrew said. "You can take Chris's room."

"I was thinking I would be at Chris and Cassidy's?" their mom asked, and Brian held up his hands.

"Nope, I'm out." Brian made Andrew grin. "I might be in public relations, but this is above my pay grade."

Everyone laughed, and Brian retreated, eventually finding himself minding one of the old hay bales that were kept in the barn for the community dances. As he watched, he felt a wave of sadness wash through him.

Was it that long ago that he thought he'd be in Chris's position, smiling happily and looking like a man who'd just found paradise? Was he the one teasing his little brother about being a computer nerd who'd never get a date because girls didn't like gamer geeks? That he and Simon would end up sharing an apartment and spending their twilight years playing old games and griping about how things were better in the good old days when you actually had to use controllers instead of a mind-link sci-fi system?

Now his little brother was happily married to a gorgeous bride while Brian was single. He didn't even really fit in with the rest of Saint Cloud; he hated cowboy boots and was only wearing them today because all of the men in the groom's party were.

What made it worse was that he wasn't a city boy either, not by any means. He knew that while he might have liked sports cars, Italian-cut suits for business, and basketball shoes for relaxing, he had enough "small town" ideas and values in him that he'd be just as uncomfortable in Los Angeles or New York as he was in Saint Cloud.

Probably why he was both single and comfortable in PR, he thought. On one hand, he had varied enough interests and a widely affable enough personality that he could make at least a good impression on almost anyone. But at the same time, once people were past that initial feeling, they saw that Brian ... just didn't quite fit.

He was the in-betweener, he supposed.

The music changed again, this time going a little country as Faith Hill came on. Brian was surprised when his mother came over, smiling. "Would you, honey?"

"You sure, Mom?" he asked, and she nodded. "Well, then, why not?"

Brian took her hand as they started to dance.

"This brings back memories," she said quietly, sadness and nostalgia tinging her words. "Your father and I would dance to stuff like this. More Dolly Parton than Faith Hill, but I don't want to seem that old."

"You're hardly old, Mom," Brian said. "Some days you seem younger than I am."

His mom rolled her eyes. "You always have been a flatterer. Now let me be a mother for a minute and ask you just why in the world you're holding up the side of the barn instead of dancing with a pretty lady?"

"I am dancing with a pretty lady."

"One your own age, and buttering me up won't get you out of this."

Brian shrugged as he turned his mother in a quarter circle turn, smiling a little. "Guess I'm just not sure who to ask."

"Well, if you ask me, that pretty girl with Simon looks like just your type," Brian's Mom said, and he looked over. Of course he'd noticed her before—Amelia Hernandez was one of Cassidy's best friends and, more importantly, a member of the Saint Cloud City Council. Her going to bat for the Davises and for Cloud 9 Games a few times had made life ten times easier for the brothers.

She was smart, Brian had no doubt about that. She hadn't worked with him directly, but he knew from Andrew and Chris how on the ball she was.

And his mother was right; she was incredibly beautiful. Her long, raven's-wing-black hair hung halfway down her back, her lean, slightly angular face so perfectly balanced and proportioned as to make her look almost artistic. And in her dress, she was … well, elegant and beautiful.

"I can see that look, Brian," his mother said, and he pulled his eyes away. "Are you seeing her for the first time?"

"Nah. Do you know her nickname is Dawn Quixote?" Brian sighed. "I seriously doubt we'd get along. Just from what Chris has told me, we'd be like oil and water. It is what it is, Mom."

"Uh-huh," she said, and Brian bristled, making his mother smile. "Uh-huh."

Brian just laughed. "Come on, Mom, let me give you a big dip before the song's over."

"Okay." His mother thankfully let the matter drop. "But if you go too fast you might break my back."

"You know," Brian prepared for the big twirl and dip, "they've got yoga classes for that."

She laughed. "You sure you're aware of where you are, Brian?"

He was perfectly aware. He was about six feet from Amelia.

Who really was gorgeous.

———

Get Cloudy with a Chance of Billionaire.